PRAISE FOR

Holding Her Breath

"Ryan's writing is quick and understated and addictive, and the story offers points of entry for many readers—competitive athletes, people who love literary drama, anyone who felt unmoored and different in college."

—*Glamour*

"From the first sentence to the last, this is a great piece of writing—precise, sure, engaging, and a joy to read."

—Roddy Doyle, Booker Prize–winning author of *Paddy Clarke Ha Ha Ha* and *Love*

"An assured, absorbing first novel that follows a young woman as she begins the delicate work of finding out who she is and where she stands in relation to her history. . . . A crisply written, empathetic novel. Ryan offers a realistic, perceptive view of the early college years, reflecting how difficult but liberating the first steps to adulthood can be. An absorbing, nuanced coming-of-age novel."

—*Kirkus Reviews*

"Ryan's debut is a joy to read. . . . Emotional, clever, and humorous, *Holding Her Breath* will engross readers with its academic atmosphere and family drama."

—*Booklist*

"Eimear Ryan expertly renders a lionhearted protagonist's attempt to escape her family's long and hurtful shadow. Patient and searing storytelling at its best. *Holding Her Breath* announces the arrival of an unforgettab̶l̶e̶

ie-Helene Bertino, author of *Parakeet*

"An Irish collegiate swimmer unearths the truth about her grandfather, a famous poet, in Ryan's penetrating debut. . . . Readers will want to see what Ryan does next." —*Publishers Weekly*

"*Holding Her Breath* does not feel like a debut novel; it shows the deft assurance of someone who has spent years training for this. . . . A sparsely written, emotionally affecting coming-of-age story. . . . Feels entirely fresh." —*Irish Times*

"Explores love, desire, and the secrets of the past with the background of student life. And it does so deftly, with complex, but fully realized characters; and is so accomplished, so wonderfully written and thought through, that it's hard to imagine it's a debut at all. I absolutely loved it." —*Irish Examiner*

"Ryan's depiction of starting college, making friends and embarking on your first real romance is very assured, and she handles the familial and friendship dynamics very well. The mystery of the family narrative drives the plot, culminating in a satisfying ending. A refreshing, accomplished debut." —*Irish Independent*

"Written with a wonderful clarity and insight, *Holding Her Breath* lingers in the imagination. Beth's unraveling and re-raveling is drawn with great skill and empathy. A brilliant debut."
—Donal Ryan, Booker Prize–nominated author of *Strange Flowers*

"A compelling look at coming-of-age concerns beneath the taboo of generational mental illness. . . . An engaging, sensitive story set in Ireland, sure to resonate with readers far and wide."
—New York Journal of Books

Holding Her Breath

Holding Her Breath

A Novel

Eimear Ryan

MARINER BOOKS

New York   Boston

HarperCollins books may be purchased for educational, business, or sales promotional use. For information, please email the Special Markets Department at SPsales@harpercollins.com.

Originally published in the United Kingdom in 2021 by Sandycove, an imprint of Penguin Random House UK.

A hardcover edition of this book was published in 2022 by Mariner Books.

FIRST MARINER BOOKS PAPERBACK EDITION PUBLISHED 2023.

The Library of Congress has catalogued a previous edition as follows:

Names: Ryan, Eimear, author.
Title: Holding her breath : a novel / Eimear Ryan.
Description: First U.S. edition. | New York : Mariner Books, 2022.
Identifiers: LCCN 2021053771 (print) | LCCN 2021053772 (ebook) |
    ISBN 9780063236080 (hardcover) | ISBN 9780063236097
    (trade paperback) | ISBN 9780063236103 (ebook)
Subjects: LCGFT: Novels.
Classification: LCC PR6118.Y3544 H65 2022 (print) | LCC PR6118.Y3544
    (ebook) | DDC 823/.92—dc23
LC record available at https://lccn.loc.gov/2021053771
LC ebook record available at https://lccn.loc.gov/2021053772

ISBN 978-0-06-323609-7 (pbk.)

23 24 25 26 27 LBC 5 4 3 2 1

For Cal

Holding Her Breath

Chapter One

She has the whole pool to herself.

She has seen the others off: the rugby players in for their recovery swim, who splash around for twenty minutes and then retire to the sauna; the slow, steady pensioners who breaststroke endless laps. Beth counts them leaving, one by one, as she sluices through the water, flipping tautly at each end.

It will never leave her, she thinks: the need to win.

The DART passes on the bridge that stretches over the complex, momentarily turning the pool nightclub-dark. She breaches the surface to adjust her goggles. The lifeguard makes eye contact and then looks pointedly at his watch. She swims another five laps before getting out, her skin drum-tight.

It feels illicit somehow, being alone in the water. No coach towering over her at the pool's edge, saying surely she can do better than *that*. Now she does as she likes. After a hundred laps she feels calm and rejuvenated, her body pinging with the tremors of exercise. An old, good feeling.

She started again last winter, doubtful at first, not telling anyone. Poking the pool's calm surface with a toe as if testing a bath for temperature. But as soon as she slipped into the water she felt her body relax in a way that it hadn't in months. It wasn't the act of swimming that had been the problem, it turned out; it was everything around it. It was the specter of her potential rippling after her, impossible to shake off.

Her new on-campus apartment is opposite the sports complex. Her bedroom overlooks the climbing wall with its brightly colored footholds. This morning she sat in her window and watched. It was raining and it seemed as if the climbers were in danger of being engulfed by the rain-drops that streaked down her window. Later, she will fall asleep to the rumble of the DART and—she imagines this part, at least—the slosh of water in the dormant pool.

She crosses the street to her new home, her wet hair hardening in the autumn breeze. Her mother was hurt when Beth announced her intention to move into rooms, an hour by train up the coast from the family home. It would have been possible, she supposes, to commute—but the room came with the sports scholarship. This is a chance for independence, however fleeting, and she owes it to herself.

So far she's only had momentary glimpses of Sadie, her assigned roommate, who's perpetually on her way out to the various Orientation Week activities (*Treasure Hunt! Table Quiz! Giant Jenga!*) that Beth is too shy to attend on her own. But in some ways, they are already on intimate terms. The shower drain is thatched over with Sadie's dark red hair, the bathroom cabinet full of palettes and butters and serums that Beth can barely identify, much less apply.

Her wheelie suitcase and assorted cardboard boxes stand in a loose ring on the bedroom floor like a Neolithic monument. She considers the window, the narrow bed, the empty shelves. The room is a clean slate.

She goes into the tiny kitchen that bridges her room and Sadie's. Fills the kettle, flicks it on. Sadie's door is slightly ajar; if she shifts her weight, it might creak open.

The first thing she notices is that Sadie has moved her furniture around, managed to wrestle the room's formation into something less utilitarian. Breeze-block walls broken up with vintage posters of *Some Like It Hot* and *À Bout de Souffle*. Fat luxury candles in defiance of the stern fire safety talk they had to sit through on day one. Cushions and beanbags sprouting everywhere like colorful spores.

Beth takes a sort of pride in her own stripped-back decor. What sort of person is her roommate, that she has to advertise her personality so forcefully? A person who wears band T-shirts. A person who reads old paperbacks in public and hopes to be asked about them.

Sadie's bed is unmade, which reassures Beth somehow. She sits on the rumpled blankets to examine the built-in bookcase. Her attention is immediately drawn to a familiar bright yellow spine: Benjamin Crowe's *Selected Poems*. Absentmindedly, she pulls it out.

Most of the shelves, however, are taken up by DVDs: *The Lodger*, *Cat People*, *Gaslight*, *The Hitch-Hiker*, *Diabolique*. Unlike the books, the movies aren't alphabetized. It bothers her, an itch she wants to scratch.

The apartment door opens. She has no chance of making

it back to her room unnoticed, but she plants her feet anyway, tensed for flight. The book, incriminatingly, is still in her hand.

Half of Sadie's face is obscured by a striped scarf, which she unwinds with whirring efficiency. Her features, when they emerge, are fiercely defined: strong brows, big glasses, heavily glossed lips.

"Oh, hello, Beth," she says.

"Yes. Sorry. I came in to get . . ." *A tampon? A hair-tie?*

"Don't worry." Sadie drops her satchel on a tiny, perfect footstool. "I've creeped many bookshelves in my time. They're arranged by year, by the way, not by title or director."

"What?"

"The films. If you want to borrow any."

"Oh. Thanks." The kettle clicks off. Beth nods toward the kitchen, grateful for the cue. Sadie blocks her way.

"Stay and have a chat," she instructs.

Sadie is doing English, in a two-subject moderatorship with Film Studies. She's from Laois and her accent sounds flat to Beth, almost terse.

Sadie gestures at Beth's wet hair, her dampening T-shirt. "Are you just out of the shower?"

"I was swimming."

Sadie nods. "You've powerful shoulders on you. Here, what was your last name again? I want to add you."

Her phone is out, her fingers probing the screen. Beth says "Crowe" before she remembers how pitiful her social media presence is.

4

"Any relation to your man?" she says, gesturing toward the *Selected Poems*. Still she scrolls.

"He's my grandfather. Or was."

Sadie gapes at her. "Fuck. Off."

"Yeah, it's no big deal really. I never knew him or anything, because obviously . . ."

"It's . . . kind of a big deal? He was one of the few poets on the Leaving Cert that wasn't an absolute dose to study. 'The Sea God?' The fucking 'Sea God,' man. It destroyed me. What's your favorite of his poems?"

Beth folds her arms and looks at the ceiling, hoping to convey the difficulty of choosing. "'Skiff,' if I had to pick one? I'm not as familiar with his work as I should be, to be honest."

"That's allowed," Sadie says, leaning on her desk. "Sure you were reared on him. There was probably no getting away from him."

"Exactly." In truth, "Skiff" is the only one of her grandfather's poems that really speaks to her, because of its description of the small pointed boat: "a knife for cutting through water." The phrase sometimes pops into her head when she's swimming, like a mantra.

With Sadie, Beth's relationship to Benjamin Crowe seems to be an asset. In school, it was different. Kids mockingly recited lines from the poems within her earshot. When she objected, they'd just laugh. *Calm down, Beth. Don't off yourself.* Studious types complained about her "unfair advantage"; teachers asked her in front of everyone if Crowe would come up on the exam this year, as if she had any way of knowing.

He *had* come up, in the event. Beth had hesitated for a moment, then chosen the Elizabeth Bishop question instead.

They are lounging on the beanbags, half-watching *The Lady from Shanghai* on a retro DVD projector. At some point Sadie produces a bottle of wine from under her desk and pours them each a glass. Beth has not done much drinking in her life, and as the wine takes effect her movements feel slow and deliberate, as though she is underwater.

"So it's just you and your mam at home?" Sadie asks, after describing her own household. Though Sadie claims to be "well shot of them," to Beth, Sadie's family life sounds idyllic: dogs, farmland, precocious twin brothers.

"My gran lives with us too. In the attic." Beth realizes how that sounds, but cannot seem to rescue the sentence.

"Is that Ben's widow?" Sadie asks. "She's alive still?"

Beth nods.

"Whoa. Well, I'd probably retreat to the attic too, to be honest."

"She's definitely a bit reclusive these days."

For as long as Beth can remember, Lydia has been distrustful of outsiders. Even now, whenever a new article or seminar comes around, suggesting the usual things— alcoholism, womanizing, bouts of rage—it is curtly dismissed. "These people didn't know your grandfather," Lydia will say.

In her drunkenness, Beth becomes sentimental, and eases

the yellow-spined book from the shelf. She studies the author photo. Ben is standing, she realizes, in front of the gable end of the house he lived in, the house she grew up in—something she's never noticed before. He is wearing a thick woolen jumper, trying out a beard. Behind thin gold-rimmed glasses he's looking at the camera, through the camera, beyond it. He's looking out to sea.

Chapter Two

The year Beth was born, a rock star named Fritz Phoenix shot himself. Fritz had the sort of ambiguous beauty that made melancholy teens of all genders fall in love with him. Before he picked up the gun, Fritz signed off his suicide note with a Benjamin Crowe couplet. Lydia, mildly spooked by the resulting bump in royalties, set up a bank account in her new granddaughter's name. Over the years, the money had funded her swimming career: coaching, physiotherapy, equipment, travel to meets in Europe. And, for the past couple of years, regular psychotherapy.

Beth is in the car with her mother when Fritz's nasal growl comes out of the speakers. Alice switches off the radio with a flick of the driver's-side volume controls. "I'm not a big fan of that one."

"You know, Mum—that therapist . . . I think I've got as much out of him as I'm going to get." He always takes her coat, like a butler, and gestures open-handed toward the armchair, the bottle of water, the cheerily patterned box of tissues. "So I was thinking of finding a new one, closer to college? And Fritz can pay for it."

Sadie has taken Beth's early intrusion as tacit permission to pop into Beth's room unannounced any time she likes. She is constantly borrowing and lending. She finishes Beth's milk and puts the empty carton back in the fridge. In the mornings she hands over her scarf or her Ray-Bans, insisting they look better on Beth, anyway.

Beth quickly settles into a routine. She is only required to train with the university swim team three evenings a week, and supplements this with gym sessions and lone swims. Breaststroke is her best race, but butterfly is her favorite. It's the most optimistic stroke, she thinks—all that power, all that extravagant splashing. She used to pretend she was swimming the English Channel, or wreck diving, or touching the wall at the Olympics. Now she just follows the dark line of tile to the opposite end, flips, repeats. Afterward, her mind is clear as an evacuated building.

Sometimes old patterns intrude. She occasionally still wakes before dawn, her body anticipating an early-morning pool session. Other habits persist: the protein- and potassium-rich breakfasts of porridge with chopped banana, scrambled eggs and chocolate milk; the reflexive refusal of chips in the dining hall.

"You eat like a convalescent," Sadie observes, watching Beth sit down to brown rice and broccoli.

Sadie is as fascinated by Beth's swim schedule as Beth is by Sadie's ability to style an effortless French braid.

"How do you do it?" she asks one evening as Beth heads out with her swim bag over her shoulder. "Do you ever just . . . want a break?"

I already had a break feels too complicated to explain. "It's easier to just stay going."

"Like a shark," Sadie says, clapping her hands. "You're like a *shark*."

Another time, apropos of nothing: "Swimming is cool. We're like, our most primitive selves in the water. Have you ever noticed how, if you just relax in the pool, you end up in the fetal position?"

"I've noticed, Sadie."

"It's like—the animal part of us is *always trying to go back to the womb*."

"Do you swim yourself?"

"Oh God, no. Sure I'm from a landlocked county. I never learned."

Beth, on the other hand, has been swimming since Alice enrolled her in a swimming class for infants. She has photos of a graduation ceremony, where they were all dressed in tiny robes and presented with rolled-up certificates they could barely hold. Alice told her that for the final exam, all the mothers had to throw their babies in the pool. She waited with her heart in her throat for Beth to kick to the surface, tiny limbs splayed, a starfish.

Sadie is rapt. "So your mother wanted you to swim from birth? Because of how your grandfather . . . ?"

"I think you're reading too much into it."

Her mother's trauma, she realizes, isn't something she ever thinks about. Ben's death always seemed Lydia's loss more than Alice's. Her mother was only twelve when he died. Beth tries to imagine losing her own father at that age, not having him around. The course and color of her life would be completely different.

There used to be an anniversary tradition. When Beth was young, Alice would bundle her up in scarf and mittens and they'd drive the few minutes up the coast to Greystones pier. Ben's ashes had been scattered there, and there was even a bench with a small brass plaque: *In memory of Benjamin Crowe*. They'd buy cheap flowers in a petrol station along the way and toss them into the water. Alice would say a quick prayer.

Back then, Grandad the Poet was a mythical figure to Beth. She was still in primary school the last time they'd marked the date. She was just starting to win competitions, and insisted on wearing the cheap medals around her neck wherever she went, like a tiny, power-drunk general. The memory is so vivid that it could easily be invention. She can't remember why the tradition stopped.

"So, what brings you here today?"

"I needed a fresh start, I guess. My old therapist . . . he was grand, but he was on nodding terms with my mother. We ran into him in the local Centra once."

"Too close for comfort?"

"A bit. And I've moved out now—I'm living on campus, so it seemed to make sense."

"What are you studying, out of interest?"

"Psychology."

"I'd better be on my toes in that case. But I suppose my question was more along the lines of—what do you hope to get out of these sessions?"

"That's a big question. To talk, I guess. To talk honestly."

"Are there people in your life you can talk honestly with?"

"It's hard to be honest with your parents when they're still actively trying to mold you. And . . . I don't know. I'm probably not great at articulating how I feel about things."

"You're doing well so far."

"It's different here. You're a professional."

"Talking about feelings with others—with family and friends—is that something you'd like to be able to do?"

"Maybe? Ideally, yeah. But it's hard to be . . . what's the word? It doesn't come easily. Like, I spent years swimming competitively, to a pretty high level. You learn to—you're encouraged to—push through discomfort. To not make a big deal about it, because everyone around you is going through the exact same thing. Which is good and bad, I guess. After a while, it just becomes part of you."

"What does?"

"The hardness."

She stays so long in the library reading about Gestalt proximity that she is almost late for training. In the changing room, she has just enough time to skin out of her leggings and snap her goggles to her forehead before diving in. It's no harm, she thinks; she hates the small talk of the changing room, sitting shivering until the group collectively agrees that it's time to brave the water.

The first proper taste of chlorine is both alien and comforting. To her surprise she sees Marina Quinn in the water, chatting with another swimmer. She strokes over to them.

Marina's eyes widen a little as Beth pulls alongside them. "Beth! How *are* you?"

Is it Beth's imagination, or is her tone a little too bright? "Hey, Marina. Wasn't expecting to see you here."

"I could say the same to you! I'm in second year now. Physiotherapy?"

"I know, I just meant . . . is the elite squad not keeping you busy?"

"Ah, yeah, but I show up here when I can. And it's great to see *you* back in action!" Marina's hand breaks the surface to pat her on the shoulder. "There were so many rumors and I wasn't sure whether to text you, or just give you space, you know?"

"Rumors? Do tell."

"I've said too much!" Marina laughs, and so Beth does too: it's easier. Theirs has always been a brittle friendship, ever since they joined the swim club at age eight. She, Marina and Cormac Deasy were the stars of their age group, and Pearse's pride and joy. Having her dad as her coach made Beth look on the team almost as a family, with Cormac and Marina her quasi-siblings. They grew up together in the pool, pushing each other on.

Not only were Beth and Marina neck-and-neck in the water, but the summer they were fifteen, they passed Cormac back and forth between them like a sparkly going-out top. For Beth, Cormac was a way to try out her new grown-up feelings, to break them in. She cried hot, bitter tears; she barely slept; she identified with pop songs. But even at the time, as she vied desperately for Cormac's attention, she suspected it wasn't him she truly wanted to impress, but Marina.

Beth finds herself avoiding her throughout the session. She doesn't need to measure herself against Marina any more, she tells herself. She's left that toxic, frantic realm, where Marina used to shake with rage after losing a race. Instead she observes Marina's efficient whirring style from afar, and gravitates toward her new teammates, whose names she struggles to remember but who all seem nice enough. If they know about her past, they don't hold it against her—not to her face, anyway.

They finish with a burst of sprints, and Marina ends up in the lane next to her. They are all pushing for the wall, checking the lanes to their left and right. Marina is on her shoulder. *Funnel*, she tells herself: *funnel funnel funnel*. It's her father's word: she hears it in his voice. It triggers something in her, and she knifes through the water. Her legs are burning, flooded with lactic acid. She touches the wall a split second before Marina. It doesn't mean anything—this is just training—but she has to chew the insides of her cheeks to suppress her smile.

Sadie wants to take her to a party, but she is happily engrossed by a marathon of *Serial Killer Deathmatch*.

"You watch too much true-crime shite." Sadie lunges across the bed in an attempt to close the laptop.

"It's not shite." Not for the first time, Beth explains the premise. "So, okay, these psychologists pit famous serial killers against each other in speculative death-match scenarios—"

"No, you're right, that sounds normal and fine."

Beth cradles the laptop, straining to catch the climax of the episode, an old favorite, in which Bundy uses his good looks and charm to overcome Dahmer, only to be blind-sided by Gacy. Sadie finally wrests it from her and snaps the lid shut.

"C'mon with me, would ya. There'll be free wine."

"I told you, I don't usually drink."

"And I don't usually shift the face off my fellow under-graduates, but there's a time and a place for everything."

The party turns out to be the launch of a novel by the head of the English department. The book is eight hundred pages long and deliberately obtuse, according to Sadie.

"So you've read it?" Beth asks.

"Oh God, no. That's just what Justin Kelleher said." Beth takes note of the alteration in Sadie's demeanor when she says this name, the conspiratorial drop in her voice when she mentions the seminar he's teaching.

"I can already tell it's going to be life-changing. He's a Ben Crowe specialist, too."

"Of course he is." She has a sudden flashback to last year—prepping for the Leaving Cert, her second go-round. Increasingly surreal English classes spent mining her grand-father's work for style and themes, only this time without her friends around to gently slag her and lighten the mood. *Cosmology. Religious Imagery. Loneliness and Despair.*

One group of emo kids even tried to induct her into their reading group, which she soon discovered they called the Suicide Book Club. As they discussed the canon's starry self-annihilations—Zweig, Plath, Hemingway, Mishima,

Woolf—they coughed their way through naggins of whiskey and skinny joints. Beth went along a few times, because she'd never smoked weed before and because some of the boys were kind of cute. But she felt like a fraud among them—she wasn't even sure if she *liked* poetry. When they started asking her about the particulars of Ben's death, the whys and wherefores, she began to distance herself.

"No one knows why." This was as close to the truth as she could get, but their doubtful expressions made her feel as if she was lying. "There was no note."

The launch is being held in a small art gallery, a sunken white box of a room on the edge of campus. She recognizes it as the place she took refuge one afternoon during orientation, trying to escape her classmates. They all seemed to have clustered into groups already, whispering and walking in synchrony, emitting bursts of laughter that Beth assumed were directed at her. She ducked into the gallery and pressed her forehead against the cool white wall.

It was quiet that day—just her and the kind attendants who averted their eyes and read their books as she discreetly panicked in the corner. Now the open space is filled with a phalanx of fold-out chairs. The crowd ignores the seating, gathering around the drinks table. Beth decides to make herself useful, burrowing into the scrum of bodies and emerging with two plastic tumblers of wine, only some of which sloshes onto her knuckles. Sadie seems to know everyone.

"You can go mingle, you know," Beth tells her. "Don't let me hold you back."

"Don't be silly. I brought you, I can't abandon you."

Somebody somewhere has a real glass, and pings a fork against it for quiet. A dark, wiry man in his midtwenties steps up to the microphone. He has neatly combed hair and restless eyes. She can see them swivel and dart, even at a distance. His voice is warm and sleepy, in contrast to his urgent, gesturing hands. He makes an effusive toast to the author, calling him "the soundest supervisor a stressed-out Ph.D. student could ask for."

Beth leans into Sadie. "Is that . . . ?"

Justin Kelleher, mouths Sadie, her eyes never leaving him. "He's hot, obviously."

Beth doesn't find it obvious at all, which is not to say that Justin Kelleher isn't attractive. He reminds her of a minor character in one of the BBC period dramas that Lydia loves—the deceptive colonel, perhaps, or the spendthrift vicar. As he introduces a semifamous novelist to launch the book, there is something about the way that he leans into the mic, like he's confiding to the entire room, that commands her attention. She cannot shake the feeling that she has met him before.

When the launch speech and the author's reading are done, the room audibly sags with relief. The queue for the wine table is already much longer than the one forming for the book signing.

"Have you thought about volunteering for the suicide hotline?" Sadie asks. "Some of my psych friends do that."

Beth wonders how Sadie has already managed to acquire "psych friends" when she herself, despite actually being enrolled in the course, has none. And she finds the question jarring. But she tries to roll with it. "Nah. I mean, Ted Bundy worked at a suicide hotline. You can't trust those people."

Sadie laughs crisp and clear, and now Beth sees who this performance is for: Justin Kelleher is within earshot, working the room.

"Oh, hi, Sadie." His voice is warm and quiet as smoke. "I'm impressed you're still standing."

"He went on for a while, all right." Sadie is flushed with pleasure, thrilled that Justin Kelleher knows her name, her face.

Beth pretends to sip her wine. She can feel Justin's gaze flick over to her, quick as a forked tongue.

"Oh, sorry," Sadie says eventually. "This is my roommate, Beth."

Justin shakes Beth's hand and holds on, as if trying to divine something.

"Beth Crowe," Sadie adds meaningfully. "She's Benjamin Crowe's granddaughter, isn't that wild? I'm living with literary royalty, like."

Suddenly Beth knows why she recognizes him: he visited their home a couple of years ago. It was a big deal at the time, as Lydia generally had nothing to do with academics who wanted access to Ben's archive.

They had agreed on the drill. Alice was to greet him at the door, then usher him up to the attic, where Lydia would be ostentatiously typing at her desk or reading at her window seat. They were to be left alone for a couple of hours, then Beth was to bring tea and biscuits around three. Beth remembers hearing Lydia's hacking laugh from the attic as she carefully carried the tray up the spiral staircase. She didn't take much notice of Justin Kelleher at the time—just that he seemed young and earnest, and not at all like the "vultures" that Lydia described as pestering her for interviews and access. She asked Lydia later how it had gone.

"Oh, fine. Ambitious boy. Politic."

"What was he after?"

Lydia made a dismissive gesture. "Same thing they always want—access to the archives. No doubt fantasizing about stumbling on your grandfather's diaries or a 'goodbye, cruel world' note or what have you. A grand explanation."

"So did you . . . ?"

"Oh, not a hope." She tried to grin, but Beth could tell she was exhausted. "Tell 'em a few anecdotes, pawn them off with a few letters to lesser poets, feign a bit of doddering— sure, they can't complain."

Now Justin Kelleher is smirking at her, and she knows he's remembering that same afternoon. "We've met before, haven't we, Beth? How is Lydia these days?"

Beth matches his cool tone. "Flying it. Same old Lydia."

"She'd be what, now? Eighty?"

"Seventy-nine."

He grins his sharp, white smile. "I thought we got on famously. But when I rang to arrange a follow-up meeting, she told me she was—and I quote—'banjaxed' and wasn't able to receive anyone."

Beth bites down on her smirk. "She has her good days and her bad days."

"Well, give her my best."

Sadie burbles, "Your speech was great!"

Beth, finding herself suddenly annoyed, asks Justin, "Why did you do it?"

He turns, a trace of puzzlement now folded into the smile. "I'm sorry?"

"If you hated the book, why did you launch it? If you thought it was 'deliberately obtuse?'"

She is not sure why she's doing this. The invocation of Lydia seems to have emboldened her. Sadie looks at her as if seeing her for the first time, a smile pasted in place. The silence is thin and sharp. It stretches on.

Then Justin Kelleher starts to laugh. It is, surprisingly, a warm and unselfconscious laugh. "Lydia wouldn't stand for any of my bullshit either. It must be genetic. But in my own defense: I didn't actually launch the book. I didn't say anything I don't believe. I volunteered to be the MC because I respect the man. And I owe him a lot. Does that make sense?"

"Perfect sense," says Sadie, eager to rescue the situation.

Justin smiles at them both. But before he walks away, he gives Beth a long, measuring look. She feels a fleeting surge, like lifting an empty carton she expected to be full.

"You take after him, you know," he says. "You have his mouth."

Sadie is annoyed with her on the walk home. "He told me that in confidence."

"What?"

"That he thought the novel was deliberately obtuse."

"I thought he announced it to the class."

"Yes, but in confidence!"

When they get home, Sadie puts on a lush sixties film in Swedish, glaring at the subtitles. She keeps drinking, filling her glass from the supply of Aldi Merlot she keeps under her desk, the bottles lined up like bowling pins. Beth keeps a wary watch from the kitchenette. When Sadie passes out, Beth coaxes her awake to take out her contacts. She helps her to the tiny shared bathroom, pours the lens solution into the little figure-of-eight-shaped container.

"He was flirting with you," Sadie says, her finger in her eye.

"Hush, Sades, it wasn't like that." But there is a part of her that wonders. People who've just met, in her experience, do not generally go around commenting on the shape of each other's mouths.

Eventually, Beth gets Sadie out of her shoes and into her bed. The anger has passed; she is compliant and floppy now.

"You have his mouth," Sadie murmurs as Beth turns off the light.

"Night, Sadie."

"You have his mouth!" Sadie yells, then bursts into unsteady laughter. Beth can still hear her through two closed doors.

Chapter Three

Beth told her father she would meet him at the pool after his Friday session with the local kids. Walking into the lobby of the leisure center makes her feel old, somehow; she has been coming to this pool such a long time.

Cormac Deasy still does the occasional shift here as a lifeguard, so she keeps an eye out for him, but he's not on this evening. She takes a seat in the back of the viewing area and watches her father at work: the shaved dome of his scalp, the gently hooked nose she inherited, the pitiless stopwatch in his hand. The whistle shrieks and the kids propel themselves in a shoal to the edge of the pool where Pearse stands. He splits them into groups, directs them into lanes. She knows his drills inside out.

Beth has no memories of living with her father, and sometimes she feels as though she first got to really know him at the pool. Her parents split early enough that Alice could change Beth's surname to Crowe without anyone noticing. Pearse would manifest at weekends and school breaks, usually bearing a button accordion or a hurley or a pair of soft-sole dancing shoes. When it became apparent that Beth wasn't interested in pursuing any of Pearse's passions—when she started spending every spare minute in the pool—he began studying to become an accredited swimming coach.

They learned together. Part of what made Pearse such a good coach, Beth thinks, is that he wasn't a naturally brilliant swimmer himself. He'd had to strive so hard for competency that he could describe the mechanics of swimming with utter clarity.

She, on the other hand, *was* a natural. At one point in her adolescence, she realized that the adults in the club were describing her in nearly supernatural terms: *unreal, savage, unbelievable.* She progressed steadily from interclub galas to regionals to nationals. Getting up at dawn for training, slipping into the water again after school; her world became narrow, but deep. It was only when she stopped, abruptly, that she realized how tired she was.

When Beth got the call to the elite squad, leaving her childhood pool behind, Pearse was emotional. "Don't forget about us," he'd said. His vulnerability alarmed her. She'd long suspected that he became a swimming coach purely to remain close to her, not trusting her to maintain contact otherwise.

Funnel! he's shouting at his charges now, *funnel funnel funnel!,* bent at the waist, arms wheeling in a frantic front crawl as if he could propel them along by sheer force of will.

When the session is over, she waits for him in the lobby. He arrives with two paper cups, sipping from one, carefully lapping the spilled coffee from the flimsy plastic lid. His face brightens when he sees her in a way that, as always, makes her feel guilty.

He hands her a cup, apologizing in advance for the quality of its contents. She doesn't mind the vending-machine coffee; sometimes she even craves the bitter, compost taste of it. It's only an excuse, anyway—a reason to sit together for a while on the lobby's black leather couch. Their cups remain mostly untouched on the glass table in front of them.

"So," he asks. "How's college going?"

She doesn't like this question. She is still working out how she feels about it. But she tries to put together an answer.

"Psychology is not what I thought it would be. It's all . . . synapses and statistics."

"No Freud, no?"

"No Freud. No discussion of people's motivations or why they do what they do. We haven't even touched on sports yet." She thinks ruefully of the Oliver Sacks books stacked up on her bedside locker, the ones she thought would give her an edge.

Pearse doesn't look troubled or start pelting her with solutions; he just listens. He doesn't ask how training is going. He asks after Alice and Lydia, politely, like he always does.

"Tell Lydia my fuchsia is coming in great. Thank her for the cutting, will you?"

He and Lydia have always gotten quietly along, and Beth understands this to have something to do with their shared Cork background. Lydia's accent, long flattened by academe and decades away from her birthplace, reemerges when Pearse is around. Beth likes to eavesdrop on their conversations, run through with improbable slang.

After saying goodbye to her father, Beth gets back on the DART: home isn't far from the end of the line. She has missed the house. Lydia and Ben bought it as a fixer-upper in the seventies. Previous owners had added bockety extensions and a conservatory. It's a bit of a mess, but Beth loves the house's unwieldiness, how it resists her mother's attempts to impose a minimalist Nordic aesthetic.

Her mother is waiting for her in the car park of the station, giving her a tight smile and a little wave through the windscreen.

"You'll stay the weekend, won't you?" she says as Beth gets into the passenger seat. "We hardly see you anymore."

It's more of a statement than a suggestion, and impossible to refuse. Beth relishes the Saturday nights when Sadie is out on the town and she has their whole tiny place to herself. She'd love to get back to that. But her mother is insistent.

Lydia's attic bedroom tops the house like a crown on a corpulent king. Beth ends up spending the evening there, typing up her grandmother's latest project—an essay on neglected Irish women writers of the nineteenth century. Lydia dictates, sometimes from the stack of papers on her desk, sometimes from her creased hands, tattooed with Biro notes. She's ambidextrous; as soon as she fills one palm, she starts on the other, each hand with its own distinct style.

When they finish, Lydia hefts herself out of her old purple armchair and pours glasses of sherry from a tray in her window alcove. Beth wanders over to the bookshelves under the sloping ceilings, runs her hands over the familiar cracked spines. Most of the books here have a personal connection. Anthologies Lydia edited. Every issue of *Red Gate Review*, Lydia's defunct feminist literary journal. And, of course, multiple editions of every collection of poetry by Benjamin Crowe.

"So tell us," Lydia says, sitting back down with the drinks. "How's the alma mater?"

Beth wheels over an office chair so that she can sit opposite her. "You should come visit me, see for yourself."

"Ah, I'd only be hounded. Those lads in the English department are shameless. Sniffing around as if I'm about to drop dead and leave the whole archive to them." She half-nods toward the far wall, lined and stacked with aging cardboard boxes.

"You could pass for a student, Gran. You'd blend right in." Beth is only half-joking. Lydia's outfit of yellow cardigan, floral shift dress and brown brogues could easily be transplanted onto the arts students she sees stream through campus every day. Only the flesh-toned tights and glasses chain betray her.

"Ah, go 'way outta that." Lydia swats in Beth's direction with the second glass; Beth takes it, pretends to sip.

"I met your boyfriend, by the way."

"Which one?"

"Justin Kelleher. My roommate is in one of his classes. He called here a couple of years ago, didn't he?"

Lydia nods. "An aggressive young bucko, if I remember rightly. Trying to tell me my business."

"That's what you think about every academic, Gran."

"He was worse than most. Wanting me to put a 'narrative shape' on your grandfather's death, if you can believe it." Lydia adopts a deep, plummy voice. "'With respect,

Ms. Blackwood, if that's not a spouse's duty, then it's certainly an editor's.'"

Beth winces. "He said that?"

"A gobshite, but not hard to look at, in fairness to him."

"He was asking for you, anyway."

"Pay no attention to that fella. Don't tell me he's the only interesting person you've met so far?"

Beth crosses her arms. "I haven't met my future spouse yet. You and Grandad set the bar pretty high on that front."

Lydia has told Beth the story of meeting Ben a handful of times. Now that Beth thinks of it, it was a lot more scandalous than she realized as a kid—a twenty-something lecturer setting her eyes on a first-year student in the front row and deciding she had to have him.

He had that sense of newness about him, Lydia would say, in the telling. *That broad Midlands accent and that shock of russet hair. Like he literally came out of the landscape he was born into. Sitting there in the university! Of course it wouldn't have worked at all, that awkward look, if he hadn't also been a genius. That was apparent very early on. And to hear him read poetry was . . . well, he had the voice of a much older man. Like he had a lifetime's worth of sorrows lodged in his throat.*

Now, Lydia is looking at Beth, sharp-eyed. "Be careful on campus, you. That place does things to you. The cherry blossoms, the cobbles, the sense of history. A very ordinary man can look irresistible in the right context. Have your wits about you."

"Don't be worrying, Gran."

"Because more often than not these things end in tears."

"Yes, Gran."

Lydia's palm comes down hard on the table between them, rattling the glassware. "I'm serious, girl. I know what it's like to be bowled over by someone's charisma. It makes it easy to do things you know you shouldn't."

Beth reaches out a tentative hand, lays it on Lydia's arm. Her muscles are rigid beneath her yellow sleeve.

"Don't ever hitch yourself to another person, Beth. Do you know what I mean by that? I'm not saying don't have relationships. But if anyone ever refers to you as their better half, drop them, you hear? Don't let yourself become half of the whole."

"I won't." Beth doesn't know what else to say.

"Good. Good." Lydia adjusts the glasses on her nose, fumbles with the cap of the sherry bottle. She doesn't offer another drink. Beth knows she's dismissed without needing to be told.

Later, as she's going to bed, it occurs to her that she's never actually heard her grandfather's voice. She googles it— "Benjamin Crowe" + "audio"—not really expecting much. But there's a page and a half of results. She clicks, pops in her earphones.

Here he is, in full flow, reading his famous long poem "Roslyn." Voice deep and raspy, struggling up from great depths. The hitch in his voice is so croakingly alive. The lines come back to her like a nursery rhyme: *In that dark sash a comet appeared . . . trailing its afterburn . . .*

Beth closes her eyes. His voice vibrates through her. She falls asleep that way.

Chapter Four

Beth rarely has to get her keys out when she arrives back to rooms; Sadie likes to keep their apartment door propped open. There's usually a stream of tender indie-folk aching out of the speakers and a friend of Sadie's lounging on the beanbags—a different one each time, it seems. "She doesn't even drink," she hears Sadie stage-whisper one night when she sneaks into the kitchen for a cup of tea.

Some of the friends coming through their doors are, Beth soon finds out, what Sadie calls clients: girls who have come to avail of her quiet acts of grooming sorcery. She does "wedding faces" and simple but immaculate updos. She manicures nails and plucks eyebrows. Beth hears the girls sometimes, apologetic under the tweezers: *God, the state of them. Sorry about this now, they're desperate.* In response, Sadie is the consummate professional: *Oh no, they have a lovely natural line.*

"Anything you'd like done?" Sadie asks her over breakfast. "My roomie rate is competitive."

"Nah, I'm grand." Beth swallows her toast. "Why do you even do it? If you don't mind me asking. I mean, it's not like you need the money."

She'd assumed—correctly, she would later discover—that Sadie, like most of those in her circle, came from wealth.

Sadie's laugh is indignant. "Stop trying to change the subject and let me make you over. You practically live in hoodies and tracksuit pants. And don't give me that 'I'm an athlete' excuse. Does Ronaldo let that stop him? Does Serena?"

She knows Sadie is right. She's been wearing her sportswear like armor. It tells the world who she is; no need for further inquiries.

"You're not a virgin, are you, Beth?" Sadie asks companionably one evening, as Beth marathons episodes of *They Should Have Known: Serial Killers' Wives*.

She hesitates before answering. She has never had a boyfriend—Cormac came closest—and her few sexual encounters have all been with other swimmers, which hardly counts. Put a bunch of teenagers up in a hotel the night before a swim meet, and what else are they going to do? She thinks of the boys she's been with, their shaved bodies marooned on stiff hotel sheets, as hesitant and awkward in bed as they were elegant in the water.

"Only emotionally," she responds.

Some nights, Beth hears Sadie noisily fucking someone next door. The exuberance of Sadie's yelled instructions—*Grab my hair!*—makes her tense, lying on her back in the dark. This is Sadie's arena, she realizes with a twinge of admiration. This is her sport.

There are times when she no longer feels she's just playing at being a student. Sometimes in the afternoon she lingers outside the Arts Block with Sadie's crowd, watching them smoke in the cold. Sometimes she has lunch with them and listens to their confident opinions and in-jokes; other times she eats alone in the dining hall, an unread psychology book propped in front of her.

She cooks big batches of spag bol and freezes portions in Tupperware, the lurid sauce staining the plastic. She studies in quiet corners of the library. She has a favorite armchair by the window where she likes to sit with her cheap laptop on her knees and type up her essays. There is a shallow ledge outside the window on which a bird corpse has been slowly decaying for months. It's now down to feather and bone, delicately beautiful again.

She hates labs, which feel like school, but loves the mass lectures in dim auditoriums; she can disappear into the crowd. Most of her days end in the pool. It's the one place she doesn't have to change shape.

Then, before she even registers that she's been hoping to run into him again, Justin Kelleher materializes.

She's in the sauna after an evening session, letting the heat thrum into her bones. She leans back: the sear of her skin on the slatted wood reminds her every time of steak on a griddle pan.

"Beth? Is that you?" In the airless room, his voice is tinny like a newscaster's.

She is startled. The sauna is like a chapel: no one talks here. Usually, people sit as far apart as possible. But he moves down his bench so that they are diagonally opposite. Like they're friends.

"I wasn't sure it was you," he says. "Can't wear my contacts in the pool. Barely know where I'm going."

"It's me all right," she says awkwardly. "Hi."

"I was in the same lane as you, I think. Lagging behind."

She didn't see him—she never notices anyone when she's in the right mindset.

"Those flip turns are very impressive. You're like a torpedo. Do you compete?"

"I do." She leaves it at that, because what else is she going to say? *Two-time national champion, actually?* And because she doesn't want to follow where that conversation leads.

"I could tell. I always wonder—swimming at that level—is it hard on the body? I know it's a low-impact sport, but at the rate you were going out there . . ."

"I get sore all right," she says.

"Of course." He looks embarrassed for asking such a rudimentary question.

"It's a good kind of sore, though. Your body is all tired and tingly. It's how you know you've worked hard." She trails off.

"Well, it's great that you're so passionate about it."

The word reverberates in the steam. Is that what swimming is to her, a passion? Or is it just what she does, an unthinking reflex?

"What do you think about when you're swimming?"

She is wary of his questions, his interest. "What do you mean?"

"I run a little, but I always have headphones. Podcasts or whatever. But you—you must get some amount of thinking time out there." He looks at her expectantly. "It must be very Zen."

"I don't think about much of anything. I try not to think, actually. You have to trust your body to do what it's supposed to. Once you start thinking about it too much, you're in trouble." He looks like he regrets having asked, so she tags something on: "Okay, sometimes when I'm just training, my mind wanders. I imagine different scenarios."

"Oh really?"

"Yeah. About winning and stuff." She's aware she sounds juvenile and joyless, but it's not an easy thing to explain— the way the pool lends itself to fantasies.

They fall quiet. He ducks his head, swings his feet boyishly. She takes the opportunity to glance over. Bodies have become boring to her, in general. She sees them all the time without really looking. The unspoken social contract of the swimming pool is that you don't give more than a cursory glance.

In the blurry light of the sauna, he doesn't seem quite real. Without his clothes on, he seems younger. Sweat drips from his chin. There's a small tattoo on his upper arm, so dark and haphazard that she initially mistakes it for a scattering of moles. And he's hairy. The furrow in his chest sprouts dense black curls. She follows the trail of hair down to his waistband. It always looks strange to her, the hair. She's used to the boys on the team, their skin pink and tender from shaving.

She feels his eyes on her again, knows she's been caught. She looks down, thankful that her face is red from the heat anyway. Counts to ten. Risks a glance: he's smiling at her, his mouth closed. The way he looks at her is a challenge to which she wants to rise.

"I talked to my grandmother about you."

"Oh yeah?" He straightens, his hands grabbing the edge of the bench.

"Did you really say she needed to 'put a narrative shape' on Ben's death?"

"Oh, Jesus." He runs a hand quickly through his sweaty hair. "Oh, it was a few years ago. It sounds like the sort of shitty thing I would say."

She was planning on telling him how shitty it was; she feels robbed. "Well. She doesn't like you very much."

"Hah."

"She did an impression of you and everything."

"Was it good?"

She thinks back to the haughty accent Lydia affected. "Not really. But I laughed anyway."

Now Justin Kelleher does that pleasant laugh again— quiet and self-deprecating. "I deserve that. I was an ass."

"Why did you say it?"

He inches a little closer down the bench. "You have to understand. It was a major coup to even get the meeting."

Beth finds herself nodding.

"So I decided to be bold, lay it all out there. I was way too forceful. But I couldn't not ask about your grandfather's death. You can't consider the poems without the suicide, and you can't consider the suicide without the poems."

The sauna door opens, revealing two improbably large guys in O'Neills togs, full of bristly energy. "So Michelle was giving me advice about San Diego," one of them says. "All the best neighborhoods to rent in, all the best thrift stores, how to get around, all that. It's hard to get work she says but it's so worth it."

"Oh, is it hard to get work, yeah?"

"Yeah, but it's *so* worth it she says."

Justin inches even closer. His eyes never leave Beth's. "She said something to me that's always stuck with me. She said, 'I grieve for my husband, not for the poet.' When she said that, I felt so ashamed. Just . . . seeing my own fucking thoughtlessness impacting on this person I admire." He shakes his head as if to dispel the memory. "I wrote to apologize, of course, but she never responded. Can't really blame her there."

Their knees are almost touching. She can't quite look at his face, finds herself focusing on his damp thigh, within reach. One of the young guys mutters, "Jaysis, lads, get a room." His friend guffaws.

Beth recoils. "I'd better be heading on."

"Right, right." He nods quickly.

She gets to her feet and leaves. It's three quick steps to the deep end. She dives, and the water is cold and sweet on her skin.

Afterward, in the lobby of the sports complex, she is both relieved and disappointed to see no sign of him. What did she think—that he'd be waiting there for her? She is about to go outside when she spots him, bundling through the turnstile, dressed in black, hair wet and untidy. He looks around, his face expectant, even hopeful.

The moment feels charged, as if the workings of a

contraption much larger and more powerful than herself are clicking into place. She still has time to slip quietly through the revolving door before he sees her, ample time to come up with a reasonable excuse when she runs into him again. Her swimmer's instinct is always toward safety.

She goes to him.

On the walk from the pool, she keeps her swim bag between them as a buffer, lets him walk a half-step in front. Autumn is settling in and the evening is dark and damp. The cold touches her lungs and she suppresses a cough.

He nods toward a pub doorway. It's an old-fashioned stained-glass place with no TV. They sit on stools, and it's a relief not to have to look at him directly. Instead she watches his hands as he doctors his coffee—two sugars, splash of milk, vigorous stirring.

"Can I get a packet of Tayto?" She always craves strong flavors after the sensory deprivation of the pool. The barman tosses the crisps in front of her. She wonders how he has them pegged—as siblings, lovers or friends. They are none of those things.

She opens the packet out flat and places it between them. She is grateful when his hand darts out to take some. They sit there for a moment, quietly crunching.

"I feel like I've gotten a weight off my chest," he says, warming his hands on his mug. "I've never actually told anyone how disastrously that interview went. My whole Ph.D. was about their relationship as poet and editor. The interview was supposed to be the crowning glory."

"Was any of it usable?"

"Not really. I felt sick afterward, could barely listen back to the tape. Now, I bet the only person she'd give an interview to is you."

"I tried once, for an essay in Transition Year. No joy."

Justin barks out a laugh. "Not even for her own granddaughter! God, I really did a number on her."

" 'Everything you need is in the poems,' that's what she told me. She wasn't going to spoon-feed me."

He smiles, and Beth notices for the first time a small gap between his front teeth. It seems calculated, somehow— just enough of a flaw to convey a lack of vanity, but not enough to ruin his smile.

"God, what's it *like*?" he demands. "To have these . . . *giants* for grandparents?"

They both laugh, for a moment, at the silliness of his question.

"I barely even consider Ben my grandfather, actually. He never *was* a grandfather." This is something she's felt before, but never fully articulated.

"So you don't feel much of a connection to him?"

She pauses. "I do, but I feel sort of guilty, too. People think *I'm* significant, just by association."

"There's a lot of people would enjoy that."

"I'd rather be significant in my own way." She thinks of the respectful, studious way people react when they're told the connection. The way they try to dredge up a half-remembered line. "There's this reverence for him that I've never really understood."

Justin nods. "He means a lot to people."

"Yeah, but I wonder how much of that is the legend and how much is the real person. I don't know if I would've liked the person. But the legend is hard to resist. Brilliant, troubled, tragic . . ."

"Handsome, charismatic . . ." Justin catches himself. "Sorry, you're just getting the full brunt of my man-crush here."

It surprises her, the readiness with which he says this. "Handsome" isn't the first word that springs to mind when she looks at photos of Ben. Arresting, certainly. He was a big bear of a man, with a strangely cherubic face and that shock of red hair. In most photographs, his expression was one of gentle sleaze.

"I guess so. It's weird to consider your grandfather that way."

"Unless you don't really consider him your grandfather." He grins, and something unclasps inside her.

She finishes her crisps, tells him she'd better get back. As she shoulders her swim bag, he half-rises from his stool, then checks himself. She feels his eyes on her as she leaves.

The next evening, she daydreams him in the pool. The DART passes overhead, blacking out the room, and when the lights come up the other swimmers have disappeared and she is alone. She flips at the deep end and turns, and when she finishes the lap he's slouched at the shallow end, elbows on the lip of the tile, the water licking his hip bones, watching. He swims to meet her, and without a word gathers her in his arms, drinks the droplets from her neck. He braces her against the wall of the pool; underwater, his hands are light and slow on her skin.

Then the train rattles noisily and the daydream disperses, like a reflection disturbed.

Chapter Five

She's not sure if she should tell Sadie, or if there's even anything to tell.

But Sadie knows her way around boys—men—in a way that Beth does not. *There's nothing else to do in the country*, Sadie is fond of saying, *apart from the GAA. A girl needs a hobby.* She recalls her various trysts with a specificity Beth finds wholly convincing. And then there are the confident instructions—*Harder, faster!*—she hears from Sadie's room on nights when she has company. In Beth's experience, sex is just something that filters into her personal atmosphere from time to time, like weather or strange dreams. She lets it wash over her and moves on. It has never occurred to her to express preferences, or make demands.

Sadie has given her opportunities to confide. She often name-drops Justin Kelleher: the insightful things he says in class, the faculty gossip he carelessly shares. "It's 'cause he still thinks of himself as one of *us*," she says, "a student, like."

Beth tells herself she doesn't want to encroach on Sadie's turf, imagined or otherwise. But that's not it exactly. That evening with Justin feels like a small, fragile thing. Beth likes to stoke it, to turn it over in her mind at night. Speaking of it might render it silly or worse, unremarkable. It could cause the whole thing to collapse.

*

Reading Week takes her away from the university, and the relief is exquisite. She has been imagining herself on a movie set, walking around campus as if viewed through a lens. Justin could approach from any angle at any time, and she wants to be ready.

Home is easier. Lydia has a heavy cold and spends most of the week in the attic, sitting upright in her nightie, emitting loud hacking coughs and raging at the indignity of being bedbound. Beth runs errands for her, cooks dinner with her mother, and watches reruns of *I Survived a Spree Killer*. She takes long, melancholy walks through the roads surrounding the village, out to the stony beach and back again. A popular soap was shot in the village before she was born. Beth has watched the opening credits on YouTube, with its helicopter shots of green fields and hypnotic close-ups of concrete mixers. Sometimes she sees tourists taking selfies in front of the town's Welcome sign.

One evening she goes to the local pool with the aim of unwinding, but Cormac is working, so she ends up pushing herself, stitching her way up and down the lane. It's quiet, and Cormac paces up and down in his shorts and blue T-shirt, diligently not looking at her. But she can feel his attention. She wants him to join her in the water, she realizes—to jump into the pool, shorts and all.

A group of older women come in to do aqua aerobics. She watches them for a moment: their camaraderie, their self-effacing grins as they punch foam dumbbells in the air.

Cormac opens up Beth's lane to make room for them. *Bit passive-aggressive*, she thinks. She decides to go home early.

Placing her hands flat on the deck, she propels herself out of the water and heads for the bank of lockers near the showers. She's surprised to hear the patter of flip-flops coming after her.

She turns to Cormac. "No running poolside."

He has the good grace to blush. He attempts to lean on his squeegee in a show of casualness, realizes it's not going to work, and straightens up again.

"Nice form out there. You look back to your best."

"Thanks." She smiles, genuinely pleased.

"Lots of nervous energy built up, huh? You mustn't be getting any at college."

He grins, aiming for banter, but she rolls her eyes and starts backing toward the lockers. "I'll see you later, okay?"

He looks over his shoulder quickly, then follows her.

She opens her locker and rummages for her towel, frowning when she sees him still loitering nearby.

"Jesus, Cormac. You mustn't be getting any either if you're following me around. Do the girls out in Belfield not give you a second glance, no?"

"Okay, fine. I'm still a college virgin. It's very sad. My brothers made it seem like it's nonstop riding from the minute you collect your student card."

"Classy fellas, your brothers." She bangs her locker door shut and throws her towel over her shoulder. "It's only been a month, though. I believe in you."

"What are you up to tonight?" he calls after her. She waves a shampoo bottle at him in goodbye as she heads for the showers.

There was a time when she would have lingered with him, trying to squeeze the most out of any interaction. She still finds him attractive, but his sleepy expression, which she once thought of as languid, now strikes her as vaguely dim. The realization makes her feel lighter in herself. Stronger.

He texts her the following Saturday when she's at home with Alice and Lydia. *Free gaff this weekend. The parents are away in Lourdes.* He follows it up with a winky-faced emoji.

She types back: *Oh right! I'm flavor of the month again, am I?*

She's genuinely surprised. It's been over a year since they had the opportunity or inclination—or were simply bored enough—to fuck each other.

Just a thought! It's grand if you don't want to.

Cormac's house is a bike ride and ten DART stops away. She replies that she'll be there in an hour and turns her phone off. It feels dangerous, somehow, to knock on his door without texting first to say she's outside. When he answers the door she notices, with a certain tenderness, that he has opened the top few buttons of his shirt, as if she hasn't seen his naked chest on a regular basis for the last decade.

They kiss urgently, more eager for the act itself than for each other. She tries to initiate things on Mrs. Deasy's beautifully appointed landing—plush carpet, Novena altar, fake flowers in a vase—but the condoms are in his bedroom so they stumble upstairs. With diligence, he goes down on her for approximately two and a half minutes. She tries to think of Justin as she grapples with his strong shoulders, but everything about the situation is so unmistakably Cormac—his groans, the stale dinner-plate smells of his room, the glow-in-the-dark stickers on his ceiling, unchanged from the long-ago summer when they first did this together.

They lie on their backs afterward, not looking at each other. She pats his leg in a comradely fashion.

"So I'm guessing you haven't gotten with anyone in college yet either," he says.

"There is this one guy. But it's complicated."

"Isn't it always." He props himself up on an elbow, facing her. "How are you, though? Really?"

"I'm fine, Cormac. Don't I look fine?" She tries to say this flirtatiously, echoing a line from some old movie, but it doesn't register.

"It freaked us all out, what happened. Everyone on the squad. Because if it could happen to *you*—I mean, you were the *super*star."

She wearily fumbles out of bed, starts pulling her underwear on. "Is it okay if we don't talk about this?"

He looks mortified. "I'm sorry, I didn't mean . . ."

She gives him a wan smile. "I'm just trying to move on, you know?"

He kisses her goodbye at the door, and the kiss seems so courtly, so surplus to requirements, that she's touched. He is a polite boy, she thinks, as she cycles back to the station, feeling calm and centered.

Lydia is reading by the fire when she gets home, a hot whiskey balanced on the arm of her chair. Beth is glad to see her downstairs, in her customary sheath dress. The spiral staircase is becoming more difficult for her. The heat of the fire and the smell of the cloves hit Beth as she takes off her hoodie.

"Look at you," says Lydia. "You're glowing. How was your bike ride?"

Beth sits down opposite her, warming her hands. She didn't bother showering at Cormac's and now she wonders if Lydia can tell what she's been up to. "Grand. Good to clear the head, you know?"

"Well, we kept dinner for you anyway." Lydia's smile is as pale and lovely as winter sunshine.

"I meant to tell you," Beth begins, "I ran into that Justin Kelleher fella again, just before the break."

The smile goes slack. "Oh?"

Beth launches into the story of encountering him at the pool, but minus the sexual tension. How sincere he'd been, how regretful. It feels good to get the words out.

"He kept saying how much he admires you and how badly he felt about the interview. He regrets how aggressive and rude he was."

Lydia nods. "And he wants you to pass on his apologies, is it?"

"No, that was my idea. I thought you'd be pleased."

Lydia laughs harshly. "Sorry, love. I've no interest in the self-serving repentance of an ambitious little scholarly shit."

She is used to Lydia's disdain for academics, but this is something else: real hostility. Beth eases herself out of the chair, not trusting herself to say anything further. Her mother comes in from the kitchen, holding a fresh hot whiskey.

"There's some stir-fry left in the pan, Beth."

Beth nods, a lump forming in her throat. Before she can escape to the kitchen, Alice touches the back of her hand to Beth's forehead.

"Are you okay? I hope you haven't caught Gran's dose. You look a bit flushed."

"Isn't it obvious?" Lydia's mouth is set in a grim line. "She's in *love*."

The air is crisp and blustery when Beth returns to campus. It's cold enough to wear a scarf and hat, but still so bright that the winter sun leaves an orange impression behind her eyes when she blinks. She allows herself to be buffeted along the cobbles on her way to class, red and yellow leaves sticking to her suede boots. She takes pleasure in unwinding her layers before diving into the pool. She loves that first wetting of the head; the way her environment immediately changes.

Sadie is giddy with the romance of the changing season, organizing Halloween screenings of classic horrors from her bedroom projector. Justin Kelleher's lecture on Benjamin Crowe is coming up; she suggests that Beth sit in.

"And skip developmental psychology?"

"Please, you don't even like your course."

She goes, in the end, because it's a chance to see Justin. He has developed a beard over the break—an uncertain growth patched with ginger. She wants to run her knuckles across it.

It's a big lecture hall, big enough that she won't be noticed. She sits with Sadie and her friend Jess.

"I just wanted to say your grandfather's poetry means a

lot to me," Jess says, by way of introduction. "That one poem—'Feast of the Assumption?' The really sexy one? Where he likens the Virgin Mary to Valentina Tereshkova, you know—the first female cosmonaut?"

Jess can't be any older than nineteen, but she has already transitioned effortlessly into adulthood: tasteful makeup, real leather boots, steady eye contact. Beth is mildly intimidated by her.

"Right. That one."

"That poem led me to Sappho, who I'm now, like, obsessed with. Anyway, I just wanted to—thank you, I guess? Is that weird?"

Row upon row of students are skimming through identical editions of *Roslyn*. The prizewinner, the money-spinner, the one people read from at weddings and funerals. The one Ben never saw in print.

At psych classes she's bent over her desk, scrawling words in the hope that transcription will give rise to meaning. Now she sits back, tense, nothing to occupy her.

It's thrilling to watch Justin without the pressure of him watching her back. He's at ease here in a way he wasn't in the sauna. There is a lectern with a desktop computer on which he puts up a presentation that he then proceeds to ignore, circling around the plinth for the remainder of the lecture. He is grabby with himself, planting his hands on his hips or running them through his hair. His body language seems unconscious, but it's so hypnotic that Beth begins to wonder if it's deliberate—straight out of the playbook of a seasoned politician or cult leader.

He skims through Ben Crowe's biographical details with apologies to the Irish students—"I know you probably know all this." Born in north Tipperary in 1940, son of a blacksmith. Scholarships to boarding school and university. Poetic potential discovered by the academic and editor Lydia Blackwood, whom he subsequently married. His debut collection *In a Grove* published when he was barely twenty-five.

"Though sometimes dismissed by critics as being too preoccupied with spiritual themes and, perhaps more to the point, too Catholic, *In a Grove* was actually a gentle subversion of Crowe's devout faith," Justin says. "It's a celebration of women and of folk saints: Wilgefortis, Pope Joan, Santa Muerte. The devotion to multiple figures such as these— many of them apocryphal—gives Crowe's Catholicism a decidedly pagan aspect."

Images of the folk saints appear on the overhead behind Justin. Jess stares in wonder at Wilgefortis. "That's basically Jesus with tits," she whispers.

Goldenvale followed: his obligatory nature collection, in which he romanticized and mythologized the topography of the Irish Midlands. Then, he surprised everyone with *The Lunar Fields*. In outer space, Justin explains, Crowe found the perfect combination of landscape, memory, and the celestial. *Roslyn*, the final collection, "was a culmination of everything that had come before. The very title remains a mystery. Is Roslyn an earthly place? A moon or a planet? Is it at the bottom of the ocean, as the suicide voyeurs would have us believe? Is it a mental state? Nobody knows. Sometimes Crowe writes of it as if it's a sacred place, other times a person, other times a pagan deity that would kill you as soon as cure you. I personally think it's a location, but the ambiguity is there."

"I thought it was a fictional place," Jess whispers. "A utopia-type thing."

"Isn't Roslyn an imaginary place?" It's a voice in the front row. The room animates with glances and affirming nods. This is what they were taught in secondary school, what they regurgitated in their exams.

"I don't believe it is," says Justin. "All Crowe's poetry is rooted, specific. Even if he's riffing on some mad star pattern, you can be sure he's got a specific constellation in mind. When I was an undergrad, there was a rumor that the coordinates to Roslyn were encoded within the text itself. Now, I never did figure it out—but I'll bet you a hundred euro that Crowe is talking about a real place."

"Just a hundred?" someone shouts.

"Steady on, I'm only a postdoc." Smiling tightly, Justin picks up his copy of *Roslyn*. "I'm going to give you the benefit of hearing Ben Crowe himself read the title poem. He made several recordings for RTÉ before he died. He was a brilliant performer of his own work." He trails off for a moment as he fiddles with the mouse. On the overhead, Beth can see he's navigating to the same website she visited herself recently. "There's a famous story told about a public reading he gave of 'Dark Vein'—the poem about the mental illness that's been passed down in his family. It ends with the lines 'From my mother/ and my mother's mother/ and my mother's mother's mother.' Well, there was this legendary reading in London in the late seventies where he just kept going through the generations. 'And my mother's mother's mother's mother's mother's mother's mother . . .' Went on for seventeen minutes, apparently. Ah, here we are."

Justin finds his place and turns to the class, arms crossed, as Ben's voice crackles over the sound system. Beth isn't ready. It was one thing to listen to her grandfather's poetry in private, through headphones. It feels wrong to hear him in a public setting, seeing others react and respond to his voice in real time. Heat floods her face.

At the part about the moon and the comet that Beth can never quite grasp—*And I, the spark and swarf*—Justin pauses the recording. "Does anyone know what 'swarf' means?"

"That's easy," Sadie whispers.

"Easy for a culchie, maybe," Jess replies.

Beth is fearful for a moment that Sadie will put up her hand, but the answer is harvested from the front row.

"Good, Gavin—did everyone hear that? 'Swarf' is the term for the chippings that come off a piece of metal when you're turning it on a lathe. Crowe's grandfather and father before him were blacksmiths, and he draws on that vocabulary here. The poet sees himself as the waste product of the collision of two larger bodies. In fact, he sees the entire universe as one big cosmic crucible—heat, friction, various objects striking off each other and shaping each other." Justin goes to resume the recording, then seems to think better of it. "Why do you think he has the comet 'in cahoots' with the moon? What's going on there?"

"The moon represents his madness," says a confident voice.

"That's one interpretation. Lunacy—from the Latin word *luna*, meaning moon. What else might it be?"

"A woman!" Sadie shouts.

Several heads swivel in their direction. Justin shades his eyes against the fluorescent light and peers up at them. Beth holds her breath. It's impossible to tell from the back of the room if he locks eyes with her, but somehow she feels it.

"Go on, Sadie," he says.

"The moon could be a woman. Because, you know . . . periods?"

There is a brief silence.

"Right," says Justin. "Another moon reference here. 'Menstruation' is derived from the Greek word *mene*, meaning—no prizes for guessing—moon. I know all this because my girlfriend is an accomplished linguist who also menstruates in her spare time."

It seems that the whole room laughs except for Beth.

"There are two main readings of the themes in this poem," Justin continues. "The most popular one is that the moon represents the poet's madness, and the comet? Beautiful, unexpected, fiery destruction. This reading is common among those who would seek an explanation for Crowe's death. But I tend to agree with the second interpretation of the comet and the moon, which is that Crowe was talking not about lunacy or destruction but about the women in his life—the heavenly bodies, if you will."

"He's right. This whole book is pure filth," whispers Jess. "And I mean that in the best possible way, Beth."

"Of course, there are no right answers," Justin says. "What we're doing here is interpretation. You can, within reason, believe what you like. But let's look at the passage again, specifically those lines about the moon and the comet in cahoots. What does it remind you of?" He looks from one face to another, daring them to have a go. "I'll take anything. Within reason."

Jess makes a face, bracing herself for mockery. "'Hey Diddle Diddle?'"

A few snickers scatter through the room.

"Go on," says Justin.

"Well, I suppose the reference to the moon reminded me. And the cahoots part . . . it made me think of, you know, of the dish running away with the spoon."

"Exactly," says Justin. "There are allusions to fairy tales and nursery rhymes all throughout *Roslyn*. And the register shifts between the playful and joyful, the high-minded and serious. Sometimes only his public readings gave away his jokes. He'd start laughing away at some allusion or half-rhyme he thought was hilarious. Let's listen to more of the recording, shall we?"

Beth shuts her eyes tightly. Ben's voice washes over them all, and again she is mortified without quite knowing why. She thinks of the misery of going through her grandfather's work in school, how she would keep her head down in class and hope that there wouldn't be too much anguish or sex in that day's poem, bracing herself for her classmates' sniggers. The rapturous reception in this room is the other extreme. Her head is spinning.

Class is about to wrap up when a boy in the front row puts up his hand. "Just wondering—when are we gonna talk about his death?"

"What's that, David?"

"His death. The way it's foreshadowed all throughout *Roslyn*."

"Is it?"

The boy called David seems annoyed. "Of course. How does Julie Conlon-Hayes refer to it? 'Western literature's most moving suicide note.' He killed himself before it was even published. This book—it's his *Ariel*, basically. The writing of it drove him mad."

Sadie shoots Beth a sympathetic look.

"Fair point," says Justin. "There are many who buy into that narrative. But loath though I am to disagree with Conlon-Hayes, it should be noted that she was personally close to Crowe—very close, perhaps. And more generally, is there something problematic about reading madness into the work of a poet like Crowe—or Plath, for that matter? Because of the nature of his death, we are all the time searching his work for clues and explanations. But perhaps we should consider the poems simply on their own merits."

Beth nearly opens her mouth to object. What had he told her in the sauna?

"But surely the context in which they're written is relevant," argues David.

"Fair enough. Of course, Crowe was disturbed in the last year of his life. But then, poetry can't be all inspiration and transcendence. Crowe's genius is that through language, he transforms these darker poetic visions into something fierce and compelling. Something to be confronted—admired even—rather than feared."

"But is that not just romanticizing mental illness? It's grand if you kill yourself as long as you get some good poems out of it first?"

"Look—I've been where you've been, believe me. It's a compelling story. It's tempting to look on these poems as a cry for help, or the outpourings of a disturbed mind, or whatever. That's very romantic. The 'if only's of it all. But that reading, in my opinion, does the poems a disservice. Crowe, most generously, *invites us in* to his mental turmoil—controls it for the reader, mediates it. It's an act of faith, and the best way we readers can repay that faith, in my opinion, is by not jumping to judgment. By avoiding the rather condescending conclusion that Crowe was somehow unhinged when he wrote this masterwork."

"Even if he killed himself just after finishing the manuscript," David says flatly.

"Even then. The art doesn't answer the questions raised by the life, or indeed the death. We can force it to, if we like—Crowe isn't around to interpret his work for us, and his wife, Lydia Blackwood, is fiercely protective of his archives and doesn't speak publicly about him. Any speculation about his suicide would be just that. We must let the poems stand alone."

You can't consider the poems without the suicide, and you can't consider the suicide without the poems. That was what he'd said to her.

*

Afterward, all Beth wants to do is call her mother and possibly take a nap, but Sadie invites Jess back to their place. "Let's hang out in your room for a change," Sadie says, unlocking the front door.

They stand in the middle of her room: laundry basket spewing gym gear, desk a jumble of dirty coffee cups and printouts, bed rumpled, a scent of chlorine.

"Cozy." Jess sits on the deep windowsill, the only viable seat in the room, while Beth smooths out the duvet. "Oh wow. Those guys on the climbing wall look like ants."

Sadie starts to make tea, but before the kettle is boiled she thinks better of it and returns with a bottle of wine. She thoughtfully pours a slightly smaller amount for Beth. Beth swirls the wine around the bowl of the glass, enjoying the way it leaves a trail.

"So did you learn anything you didn't already know?" Jess asks.

"I did, actually."

"They don't talk about him at home," Sadie says.

"Ah, we do," Beth says. "When Gran is in form for it. Which isn't often, admittedly but . . . I mean, how often do *you* guys talk about your dead ancestors?" She drinks, swishes the wine over her gums, registers the slight check of nausea.

"Is it still painful for her, then?" Jess asks.

Beth thinks of Lydia's hand smacking down on the table between them. "She's never gotten over it."

Sadie transfers some of Beth's clothes from the armchair to the table, then sits down cross-legged. "How did you even find out about him? As a kid, like. How was it explained to you?"

Beth looks at the floor. The attention is intense, but also pleasurable. "I was told he drowned. When I was a bit older, my mother sat me down and gave me the truth. It was the first I'd ever heard about suicide."

"How old were you?"

"Eight or nine. I accepted it, I think. You do when you're small, right? Even if you don't fully understand."

Jess nods. "How cringey was David, though? Fixating on the death. Not classy."

"I actually disagree with Justin Kelleher on that point," Sadie interjects. "The suicide is important. Especially through a feminist lens."

"Oh, this'll be good," Jess says. "Go ahead, Sades— femsplain Ben Crowe's death to his actual family member."

Sadie falters a little. "Sorry, Beth. I'm not trying to be a dick. But, like, I've always seen him as a feminist icon."

Beth laughs. "Seriously?"

"Yes! The way he writes about women, it's . . . wonderful. There's no ego in it, no objectification. But it still manages to be really sexy, I don't know how he does it. And"— she drops her voice—"his death feeds into the feminist vibe. Suicide by water is coded female. Virginia Woolf . . . Ophelia, for God's sake."

Jess pipes up, warming to Sadie's argument. "There's also the way he identifies with the troubled female line in his ancestry. 'My mother's mother's mother' and all that."

"Or *blames* the women in his family," Beth says.

"Holy shit, Beth." Jess, idly fiddling with the items on Beth's desk, has picked up her student card and is examining it. "You're a mature student!"

"What?" Sadie sounds betrayed. "*How* mature?"

"I'm only twenty," says Beth. "Just gone. In September."

"I won't even be nineteen until April!"

"It's not a competition, Sades."

"Did you take a gap year or what?" Jess asks.

It would be easy to lie now; say she went off volunteering somewhere, or took a year out for her sport. But she wants to keep these friends, would rather not have to remember a series of elaborate inventions.

"I had a bit of a crisis the spring before my Leaving Cert," she says, keeping it as vague as possible. "Made an absolute hames of it, so I had to repeat. My parents were freaking."

"Stop," says Jess. "At least you're not still living with your folks. My mum loses it if I go somewhere and don't immediately text on arrival. Just straight-up assumes I've been murdered."

"The statistics on stranger danger might surprise you, actually."

They laugh, and Beth exhales, feeling she has passed some kind of test.

"So where's Roslyn, then?"

It's evening, they are drunk, and Beth has asked this question aloud without quite meaning to.

Jess smiles. "We were hoping you'd know the answer to that one."

"Nope. I learned the same thing in school as you did. Imaginary."

Sadie pulls her phone out of her back pocket, types rapidly. "Okay . . . according to the internet, it's from the Irish *ros linn*, or 'the wood by the lake.' Thought to be the name of a now-defunct townland near where Crowe grew up. Although . . ." She scrolls furiously, the screen reflected in her lenses as squares of light. "This other page has a whole *Citizen Kane* theory."

"Roslyn is not a sled," Jess says firmly.

"No—they're speculating it was the name of a boat he had during childhood. He grew up near Lough Derg, right? They say here it's the same boat that 'Skiff' is written about."

"Roslyn is not a boat," says Jess. "Roslyn's not a vessel or vehicle of any kind, just get that idea out of your systems."

"And this *other* source says it's not a place at all, it's a woman's name, and *she's* his metaphorical home—sorry, Beth."

"It's not that one, anyway," says Beth. "Lydia's no fool. She'd have noticed if he was sleeping with someone named Roslyn and then writing poems about it. She'd have put two and two together."

Sadie refills their glasses and Beth feels lit up inside. She speaks louder, becomes surer in her opinions. She eats nuts from a communal bowl by the fistful, licks her fingers clean of the salt. A name comes back to her from the lecture, needling her.

"Who's Julie Conlon-Something?" she asks.

"Julie Conlon-Hayes?"

"Yeah. She said that thing about 'Western literature's most moving suicide note.'"

"She's a feminist critic," says Jess. "I've read her essay about Crowe, the one David quoted. She's interesting."

"And Justin Kelleher said she was close to Ben."

The conversation moves on to other things, but Beth's mind keeps circling back to Julie Conlon-Hayes. When she wakes in the middle of the night, hangover already under way, she picks up her phone for distraction.

The Wikipedia entry is as brief as a book jacket blurb. *Born 1948*, it reads. *Julie Conlon-Hayes is an Irish essayist and literary biographer. Notable works include* The Constant Reader: A Life of Dorothy Parker *and* Comely Maidens: Discourses of Female Desire in Irish Literature. *She lives in West Cork.*

Chapter Six

Sadie comes into her room in costume: body-hugging U.S. Army uniform and old Hollywood hair, curled and blown out.

Beth takes a stab at it. "Sexy soldier?"

"Excuse yourself. You think I went to the sexy aisle at Party Planet?"

"I'm just . . . genuinely at a loss here. And you do look sexy."

"Thanks, hon. I'm Marlene Dietrich. To be honest I just dressed like this as an excuse to go around shifting everyone, which is what Marlene did during the liberation of Paris."

When Jess shows up in jeans and a T-shirt, saying she ran out of time, Sadie produces a dipping Morticia Addams dress from her wardrobe. She sits Jess in her spinning desk chair and conjures cheekbones, inkwell eyes, stark pops of blood red on her lips and nails.

"How much are you charging me?" Jess asks.

"This one's a freebie."

They twirl for Beth's inspection. The long-sleeved dress billows from Jess's body like a plume of smoke.

"Now, Beth," says Jess. "Are you sure you don't want to come?"

Beth has already expressed her determination not to attend the LitSoc Halloween party. "I'll only end up drinking. Again. You two are a bad influence. Anyway, I've training tonight."

"You have training every night." This, accusingly, from Sadie.

As soon as they're gone, Beth checks that Sadie's hair straightener is unplugged, packs her swim bag, then double-checks the straightener. It's half an hour until the session begins but she decides to pop over to the sports complex anyway.

She slips into the pool to warm up, starting at the deep end. She dislikes the shallow end as a rule, prefers to feel the pillowy force of the water beneath her, buoying her up. After twenty laps, she treads water and watches the various ways people have of propelling themselves through the lanes. There's an older man who pounds his right fist into the water, letting his left arm drag behind like a broken limb, and a student who kicks mostly air. Her feet make a dunking sound when they break the surface, like a bucket dropped in a well.

Beth resumes her slow laps. Every so often Ben's voice comes back to her. She's been listening to him every night in bed, swapping out her usual murder podcast. His beautiful diction, selective and controlled; hints of weariness and pain with no elaboration.

You can't consider the poems without the suicide, and you can't consider the suicide without the poems. Or else: *We must let the poems stand alone.*

Someone's locker key is marooned underwater like lost treasure, its orange wristband still attached. It seems impossibly lonely and brings a lump to her throat. She is becoming sentimental, she thinks; this is the danger of poetry.

In the shower afterward, it seems to take forever to get clean, for the dense warm fog to envelop her. She rakes her nails over her arms and thighs as if scraping the chlorine off.

Marina takes the showerhead next to hers. Between lathers, they discuss upcoming meets. Marina is gearing up for the Irish Open in the summer, hopeful of a gold medal and Olympic qualification.

"You'll fly it, don't worry," Beth tells her. "You came so close the last time."

"Don't remind me." Marina unwinds her long braid and viciously hacks through her hair with her fingers. Neither of them alludes to how Beth got on last time. It feels strange to talk with detachment about something that used to dictate her every waking moment. A few years ago, their conversation would have been a frantic exchange of information, neuroses and reassurances. Now all the attention is focused on Marina, a dynamic they're both probably more comfortable with.

Then Marina broaches the topic that Beth suspects she's been building up to all along. "So what's going on with you and Cormac?"

"Nothing." Off Marina's look, she elaborates. "Nothing that hasn't previously gone on, anyway."

"Ooh. *Shenanigans*." Marina coils her hair up in a white

fluffy towel; the effect is regal. "Are you—I mean, are there feelings involved here?"

Beth considers this. She likes Cormac; how comfortable he is, how deadpan and unflappable. "General goodwill?"

"Okay. Great. Well, I just said I would check with you. I might be in need of shenanigans myself soon but didn't want to step on any toes."

"Oh, work away." Beth twists the water from her own hair.

"Thanks." Marina smiles. "How lucky is *he*? Let's be honest, we're both much better-looking than he is."

"Boys get all the breaks."

She watches Marina's retreating back, admires her stroppy elegance. She wonders if Cormac approached Marina, or if Marina is about to make a move on Cormac. She can't quite decide if she minds—which, she supposes, must indicate that she does not.

Pearse is waiting for her in the lobby of the sports center. She almost doesn't recognize him in his work suit. He's holding a giant Toblerone, which looks dangerous in his large hands. He goes in for a hug but she takes a small step back.

"Did we . . . did we say we'd meet here? I was planning to get the bus out." She spends the last weekend of every month with her father, but they haven't yet established a routine since she started college.

He shrugs. "I was working late, thought I'd collect you. Protect you from the ghosts and ghouls."

"And you brought me a weapon. Very thoughtful." She hefts the Toblerone. "How was the minibreak?"

His smile is involuntary. "Good. *Very* good."

"Okay, Dad, you can spare me the details."

He grins broader, pleased at her use of *Dad*. "Bordeaux is a fabulous city, that's all I'll say. A bit like Cork, you know? It's the Cork of France. Very walkable, very laid-back."

"And your traveling companion? Anything fabulous there?"

His cheeks go pink beneath his gray stubble. He's not used to being teased by her. "Dee is . . . a lovely woman."

"Good. She'd want to be. And when do I get to meet her?"

"Early days yet, Beth."

If her father had other relationships after the separation, he never told Beth about them. She wonders what's changed. Either the relationship with Dee is serious, or Pearse now considers her grown up enough to know about this part of his life, or both. She wonders if her mother will ever find someone; if that's something that even interests her. She imagines Alice trying to move a man into Lydia's house, and suppresses a smile.

She collects her overnight bag from her room, and they walk together to the multistory where Pearse's car is parked. Dusk is settling itself down as they reach the suburbs, and there's already a brisk footfall of tiny witches, vampires and ghosts.

Pearse has rented the two-bed redbrick terraced house for the past decade or so. The house's interior is a disarming mix of bachelor pad and the sort of decor he once thought might encourage a sullen teenage daughter to spend more time with him. In the living room, a dusty Nintendo Wii is still hooked up to the TV. Above the couch, bodhráns are arranged on the wall like battle shields.

Beth's room is still painted purple and black on alternating walls, a whim of her fifteen-year-old self. The mirror at her vanity table is draped with the heavy jewelry of her emo days: skulls, spikes, silver crosses. She had been determined to get piercings, until Pearse pointed out they'd create drag in the water.

The room has become a dumping ground for all the parts of herself she's left behind. Old swimming trophies, favorite childhood novels, posters she once thought marked her out as discerning or alternative. All the stuff she's cycled out of her primary life: it winds up here.

"Are you hungry?" Pearse calls up the stairs. "I can fire up the spiralizer."

As her father makes dinner, Beth sprawls on the sofa, her laptop balanced on her stomach. Dimly lit reconstructions of crimes flicker before her. There is something comforting about the scenery-chewing of these C-tier actors, the way they leer at their victims, almost salivating at the prospect of the kill. As if real-world monsters could be spotted so easily.

BTK's attributes include master manipulation; an ability to show one face to the world, only revealing his monstrous visage to his victims—

"What's that you're watching?"

She straightens up. Pearse is holding two full plates, his expression open and curious, as if he might join her.

"*Serial Killer Deathmatch.*" She folds her laptop, cutting off the narrator in midsentence.

But for all Rader's dark gifts, could he be any match for Aileen Wuornos, with her limitless thirst for violent retribution against sexual predat—

"Oh, don't let me interrupt. Looks like good Halloween viewing."

"I can finish it later." Her parents know that she's into "blood and guts," as Pearse calls it, but they don't know the full depths of her obsession, nor do they need to. She's not sure they would believe her if she told them that watching murderers, far from stoking her anxiety, actually helps to relieve it.

They eat at the coffee table, flipping through the movie channels' parade of slasher flicks. For dessert they break off chunks of the Toblerone.

"You seem in good shape," Pearse says, unprompted. "Much better than I anticipated."

Beth keeps her eyes on the screen, where Rose McGowan has just had her head squished in the garage door. "Do we have to talk shop?"

"I'm complimenting you! The only thing that concerns me is your underwater trajectory. You're diving too deep."

She turns to look at him. "You were watching me?"

"I just saw the last ten minutes of the session. Like I said, I'm really happy with your form overall."

She breathes deeply, counts to five before answering. He

means well, she knows. "Can you please not do that? Call in to training unannounced?"

He looks hurt. "I'm not clear on what the problem is here."

There is a strained silence. Neve Campbell is about to lose her virginity to the bad guy.

"I'm only getting back into it, Dad. I don't need—I don't want this sort of scrutiny, okay?"

He doesn't respond. They both pretend to be more engrossed in the movie than they really are. When the credits roll, they clear the plates together.

"Marina's in great form," says Pearse. "If she keeps putting in the hard graft, in a year's time . . . well, you never know."

He does not speak the word "Olympics" out loud, but she takes his meaning.

"She has the mentality, anyway," Beth allows. She does not add, *if not the talent*—that would not be quite fair. And what does talent really count for, anyway? She herself was talented, for all the good it did her.

She makes a point of phoning home on the sixteenth of November. There is never much of a to-do about Ben's anniversary. Her grandmother's atheism means no Mass. Alice and Lydia rarely acknowledge the date, and brush it off when others try.

Once, a few years back, her mother talked about her memories of the funeral. How people kept saying what a good thing it was that she was so young—too young to understand. "They said it right in front of me," she remembered. "But I understood all right."

Then and now, Beth finds it hard to picture her mother as the child she was that winter: small and quiet in a new black dress, right there on the fault line of girlhood and adolescence. The adults talking over her head.

"How are you?" she asks her mother, wincing at how insincere it sounds, the simpering inflection in her voice. Like she wants the answer to be "not great"; like she wants a dam to burst.

"Ah grand, love—thanks for asking."

"Well, I was thinking about you."

Alice nimbly turns the conversation back onto Beth—classes, friends, training schedules. When will she next be home? Are there any nice boys on the agenda? Beth deflects that one.

"Remember we used to go to the marina pier to mark the date?" Beth finally asks. "I miss that. I don't know why we stopped."

"Just got out of the habit, I suppose." Her mother sounds almost bored.

"Can I talk to Gran?" Beth thinks of the way Lydia handles the phone, wrapping the twisty old landline cord around her finger until it swells and purples, as if pinching herself to stay awake.

Alice hesitates. "She's not in great form today, and . . . well, she's dozing on and off. Best leave her be."

Beth has never known Lydia to sleep during the day. She is, resolutely, not that kind of old person.

They say their goodbyes. Beth stares at her phone a moment, absorbing the fact that even though she rang on account of Ben, neither she nor her mother was willing to say his name.

Her period starts when she's in the pool. The water washes her swimsuit clean but she can still smell it, the tang of copper cutting through the chlorine. She's been tingly recently, has sensed it coming. Her thoughts drift to sex, as they often do when she's menstruating. *Mene*, meaning moon; now she's thinking of Justin, and—disconcertingly—of Ben's poetry. She considers texting Cormac but then remembers her last conversation with Marina; best not to encroach. Besides, she's pretty sure Cormac is one of those boys who consider period sex to be out of the question.

When she gets back to her room, she puts a towel down on her bed, settles back, and rubs herself until she comes. Usually she watches something on her phone—sex scenes from glossily produced TV shows rather than porn, because the acting's marginally better. She wonders what it says about her, that she would rather watch artfully simulated sex than the real thing. This time, though, she leaves her phone on her bedside locker. She closes her eyes and thinks of being with Justin Kelleher in the sauna. If she'd closed the small space between them with a touch. Asked about his tattoo, maybe. If the two lads hadn't interrupted. If she'd lain back on the hot wooden bench, hissing from the heat. What then?

When she's finished, she feels the tension leave her body through her toes, her scalp. She goes to the bathroom. Her old tampon won't flush, and instead lurks in the water like a ghostly stingray. She resolves to run into Justin Kelleher soon, one way or another.

With a neuroscience essay due at the end of the month, she takes out a stack of books from the library, hoping that if she cites enough of them, it will distract from the gaps in her knowledge. But even as she borrows them she knows that the books will just sit on her desk for days, intimidating her with their small print and penciled notes—evidence of past students who knew what they were doing. She has started writing her own notes in the margins of her textbooks, but they're self-consciously peppy, with lots of exclamation points and doodles: a performance for her future self.

She runs into him outside the library—no stalking necessary. She feels the usual prickle along her spine and is glad to have something to do with her hands. He's all awkward chivalry, and keeps making preemptive gestures toward her armful of books. She shakes her head, smiling, although really she wants him to take them from her, to take charge of the situation. She is on the verge of doing a jokey, self-conscious shuffle in an attempt to be on her way when he stretches out his arms.

"Not to be all 'can I carry your books' but . . . can I carry your books?"

"Well. Okay." She leans forward, and he cradles the books in his arms as if receiving an infant. Accidentally, his hand brushes her breast; even through her coat, she reverberates with the touch.

"Are you gonna carry them back to my room for me?" she asks, half-teasing.

If this alarms him, he doesn't show it. "Whatever suits."

They walk toward the back of campus—rugby pitch on one side, cricket pitch on the other—not saying very much. Out on the street, she has to push the button for the zebra crossing, and they smile sheepishly at each other as they wait for the green man.

Outside the door of her building, she holds out her arms for the books.

"I can carry them upstairs if you like," he says, quietly. She is surprised by this. For a staff member to walk with her across campus is one thing; entering her residence seems different. Riskier. She wonders if people will take him for a student.

She leads the way, conscious of the fact that his eyes are level with the movement of her ass. The door is closed, meaning Sadie's not at home. She unlocks the door, shoulders it open, and tries to look like she doesn't care about the state her room's in. But she sees his restless eyes darting. He takes in the desk, covered in photocopies, folders and dirty cups; last night's workout gear abandoned on the floor. There's no obvious surface for the books to be left on.

"You can just put them on the bed," she says.

"Not the desk? Unless, you know, you're planning to sleep with them. No judgment here."

He heaves the books onto the mattress, making the bedsprings squeak.

She smiles. "Maybe I *will* sleep with them. Absorb them by osmosis."

"I think if you stare at them hard enough. And stroke them."

"That's how neuroscience works, right?"

"Well, you would know."

Her heart races at the banter, so flimsy and unsustainable. She will have to keep thinking of things to say. He places his laptop bag on the floor, where it falls heavily onto its side with a small thud. He would have kept it on his shoulder if he was in a hurry, she thinks.

"Would you like a cup of tea?" she asks.

He nods and looks around for a seat, then remains standing. She stretches out the making of the tea, stewing the teabags, making it stronger than she usually would.

"So do you often steal higher education?" he asks.

It takes her a moment to see what he's getting at. "Oh God. I could have kicked Sadie for speaking up. You'd never have spotted me otherwise."

"Oh, I'd noticed you long before that." He takes a sip of tea, winces, and she realizes she never asked him how he takes it. "So how did you find it? The lecture."

"It was interesting."

"You know, when my girlfriend says something is interesting, it means she hates it. She could be talking about a movie, an opinion column, a pale ale, doesn't matter. 'Interesting' is the kiss of death."

Her laugh is a nervous trill. "Well, you contradicted yourself. You said the poems stand alone, which isn't what you told me . . . previously." She almost said "in the sauna."

"Oh no?"

"You said you can't read the poems without contemplating the suicide or . . . something like that."

He holds her gaze for a moment and she thinks she's fundamentally misunderstood something. But eventually he says, "Okay, you got me."

"Well, which is it?"

He blows on his tea daintily before answering. "Haven't you ever held two contradictory ideas at the same time?"

"That's a cop-out." But the truth of his statement slowly lands, like an insistent drizzle. The way she both loves and resents her sport. The fact that she is both attracted to and repelled by her grandfather's legacy. The thrill and guilt she feels when watching *Lethal Lovers* and *Wives with Knives*. "Why didn't you just say that in the lecture? That you can hold both ideas at once?"

He's leaning against the door frame of the kitchenette, facing her. She finds herself mimicking his body language.

"I try to hold off on those kinds of ideas until I have to teach Blake to second years," he says. "I'd love to think the poems stand alone. That's what I *want* to believe. And I make a point of saying it to first-year students, who're more likely than most to idealize the suicide. But that's not what my gut tells me." He pauses. "Maybe this only applies to *Roslyn*. But there's this elegiac quality to it. A sense that he's racing to get those poems out of him before he dies. That thread throughout about the night sky, how the stars he's looking at no longer exist? He knew he was near death."

"He was planning it, you mean."

Justin drinks his tea. "If you track the references to the moon throughout *Roslyn* you also get a sense of a life on the wane. To begin with, in 'Feast of the Assumption,' the moon is referred to as 'round' and 'plump,' and has all sorts of erotic connotations. But later on, say in 'Crucible,' it's referred to as—"

" 'A thin rind,' " Beth finishes.

He smiles, puts his mug down on the table. "You know more of his work than you let on."

"A lot of his lines were repeated mockingly back to me by mean kids in school. It's a surprisingly effective way of committing them to memory."

"Bullying poetry into people. A new cutting-edge pedagogic method."

She laughs. "Wow. You actually had a positive school experience, didn't you."

They smile at each other. She could reach out, she thinks, he is that close.

"Thank you," she says.

"What for?"

She leans in to him. It's dark against his black shirt; orange shapes explode behind her eyelids. She can smell his detergent—floral, cheap—and under that, the ripe foodiness of his sweat. His arms, when he finally folds them around her, are tense.

She pulls back and looks into his face, still handsome

despite being confused and—she thinks—a little afraid. His mouth is slightly agape and she kisses it, forcefully, out of frustration more than anything. At first it is just a collision of mouths but then she senses him pulling back, tuning in to her. They fit so well together she almost gasps.

"You should go," she says, because that is what she's supposed to say at this juncture. She's disappointed when he actually obeys, backing away and nearly stumbling over his laptop bag. He crouches to gather it up and sling it over his shoulder.

When he turns at the door, the self-assurance is back, as if he's wiped his expression and started clean.

Beth spends a long time standing in her bedroom, worrying a finger along her lips. They are always chapped in winter; she wonders if he noticed. Her body is in emergency mode, the same as before an important race.

She begins to pace and touch the wall, pace and touch the wall. Five strides is all it takes. The grooves between the breeze-blocks accommodate her finger perfectly. Gradually, her heartbeat begins to slow. She never thought she could be one of those people to whom things actually happen. Every moment of drama or triumph in her life has taken place in the pool, and been rendered less impactful for the hours of repetitive practice that preceded it. She is not used to things happening out of the blue.

Later, she will wish they had got the sex out of the way there and then, that they hadn't left time and space for yearning to take root.

Chapter Seven

When she goes home for Christmas, the house feels strange in a way Beth can't put her finger on. It takes her a few days to realize that it's she who has changed, not the house. She has become accustomed to dorm living and doesn't quite know what to do with all the extra space. She keeps her possessions— clothes, books—in small fortlike piles around her bed. She is full of restless energy, wanting to go places and see people, but her mother and grandmother are content to stay in their routines, the repetitive loops of home. Some things she registers as if for the first time: there are very few visitors, even at Christmas; when her mother smiles, it is with a closed, tense mouth; and the bickering between Alice and Lydia, which Beth always thought of as affectionate, sometimes has a sting to it.

Living together is no longer the effortless coordinated dance it once was. When Lydia thanks her for the tea she made—*Grand cuppa, Beth!*—she snaps back, for no good reason: *It's just a cup of tea.* Quiet shock comes off Lydia in waves, and Beth can't explain her outburst; but she knows that she feels differently in this house now. The three of them wandering its rooms, all of them lost in their own way. Their inheritance of sadness in the very walls, like a toxin that they breathe day in, day out.

*

On Christmas morning, Lydia does not appear. Beth is on the couch in pajama bottoms and a reindeer jumper, worrying a tin of chocolates. At ten o'clock, Alice goes to check on Lydia.

"She's still in bed. She says to go ahead and open the presents without her."

This is unheard of. They get a breakfast tray ready—tea, toast, cocktail sausages—and haul the cache of presents from under the tree upstairs with them. Sitting on the edge of the bed, they exchange gifts. Lydia smiles sleepily, and winces when she props herself up into a seated position. Her close-cut gray hair is sticking up. Beth wants badly to smooth it, but knows the gesture would not be welcomed.

She and her mother give Lydia a blue cardigan with pockets (she insists on pockets, for her notes); a bottle of gin; a desk planner; and biographies of both Elizabeth Taylors. Lydia consigns the books to the tottering unread pile by her bed. It is higher than Beth has ever seen it.

Lydia unscrews the gin and doses the three cups of tea. "God bless us, every one!"

"But you don't believe in God, Gran."

"I believe in Dickens. Well, somewhat."

Beth is given Bluetooth headphones, a stack of Ann Rule books, a pair of boots she'd been eyeing up on ASOS and emailed to her mother, and an aerodynamic-looking travel mug. Alice receives two silk scarves, a basket of eye-wateringly fragrant bath bombs, and the box set of a Nordic crime series that Beth picked out because she wants to watch it herself.

"Aren't we doing well for ourselves," says Lydia, already tipsy.

Getting her downstairs for dinner takes a bit of coaxing. Beth leads the way on the stairs, while Alice manages her from behind. They are being newly solicitous, and Lydia doesn't like it; she shrugs off Beth's steadying arm, determined to prove she can still get around unassisted. They are all adjusting.

Beth had promised herself she wouldn't train on Christmas Day, but with her mother and Lydia arguing over basting techniques, she finds herself putting on her gym gear and lacing up her runners. She justifies it to Alice by saying she wants to try out her new headphones.

She finds herself veering toward the beach. She has never taken part in the Christmas-morning swim, but she likes the atmosphere: the supporters with towels and Santa hats and thermos flasks; the giddy shouts from the choppy, dark waves; the dripping swimmers breathless with the cold.

She has always avoided swimming in the sea. She prefers to swim within finite parameters and along well-defined lines. To Beth, the sea is for happy amateurs and shrieking children, for ferries and cargo ships and Jet Skis. The sea is for paddling, or for drowning yourself.

Still, as she watches the swimmers launch themselves off the rocks—the men's nipples red-raw in the cold, the women hugging themselves against the chill, but all of them bantering, *laughing*—she is envious.

This is the same winter cold that must have chilled Ben. Did he go shivering, laughing into the water, too?

The day after Stephen's Day, Beth receives an email—quick and to the point, as if tapped out on a phone.

Hi Beth, it's Justin Kelleher. I'm in Dun Laoghaire today— don't suppose you'd like to meet for a coffee? His signature includes a generic sign-off—*Kind regards, Justin*—as well as several letters after his name.

She imagines him accessing the student database and running a query for her email address. She makes herself wait half an hour before responding, during which time she convinces her mother to drop her to the DART station. They exchange niceties for a while—*good to hear from you, happy Christmas, yeah I overdid it on the mince pies, haha.* He is out walking the pier; she agrees to meet him at the strip of cafés overlooking the harbor.

She spots him wearing a dark wool coat and, in an apparent concession to Christmas cheer, patterned red-and-white gloves with a matching hat. Somehow, the effect is suavely festive rather than juvenile. She likes seeing how he puts himself together off campus. He raises a wool-encased hand in greeting.

"Hey." He leans forward to kiss her on the cheek, his mouth the only point of contact between their bodies. She is reminded of Cormac, dutifully kissing her at the door.

She watches for some indication of his intent, but there's nothing. The kiss in her room was so ephemeral that part of her suspects she dreamed it.

They shuffle to the nearest coffee shop. The blast of warm air as they open the door stings her face. Justin pulls off his hat, his hair snapping with static. He asks how she got over "the Christmas," as if he's an older, more rural person, and she can't decide if it's charming or contrived or both. He flirts with the barista as he orders but Beth doesn't mind; she enjoys it by proxy. It's a chance to drink him in.

The small talk lasts for the length of time it takes him to eat his slice of coffee cake. When he's finished, he puts the plate to one side and formally clasps his hands on the table in front of him, voice dropping low and confessional.

"So. I guess you know why I asked you here today," he starts.

"Not really." There's a concave feeling in her belly, similar to losing a race—an absence.

"I owe you an apology. For the kiss."

She is immensely grateful that he said "kiss," not some euphemism like "what happened" or "the incident." She laces her hands around her cup and peers into it. "I'm pretty sure I kissed you."

"That's irrelevant. I'm older and in a position of authority—well, relative authority—and it was wrong of me. I should have stopped it. I shouldn't even have been in your room, for God's sake."

His tone is so even that his meaning doesn't immediately land. When it does, she feels it in her throat.

"Don't worry about it." She tries for cool. "Lydia got up to worse shenanigans with her students, remember? You're tame by comparison."

His laugh is jagged. She takes a small measure of satisfaction from the fact that she's annoyed him. But when he speaks again his voice is gentle.

"I really am sorry. I like talking to you, and I suppose I romanticize you because of Ben. And . . . well. It shouldn't have happened."

"It's okay." She feels foolish, now, for ordering a large coffee, wanting to stretch the meeting out. Her cup is scalding and full. The silence lasts a beat too long.

"So Lydia told you about all that, huh?" he asks eventually. "The scandalous romance."

"A little." She is grateful for the conversational lifeline. "She says that's the Ben she'll always love. The innocent sitting in the front row of the lecture hall."

He leans back in his chair, becoming visibly energized on the introduction of his favorite topic, as she hoped he would. "Their relationship is fascinating. The way it changed over time, the power always shifting."

"I feel like it's still ongoing, too. She doesn't talk about him much, but when she does, it's like he's there in the room."

He smiles, and delicately lifts the cake crumbs to his mouth with the pad of his finger. "It's interesting that she has a favorite Ben. Because there were so many versions, you know? The rural boy, the scholar, the poet, the intellectual, the tortured artist . . ."

"Which is your favorite?" she asks.

He looks around conspiratorially. "*Roslyn* Ben, definitely." He shrugs off his jacket and rolls up his shirtsleeve, showing her his soft, hairless inner arm. There's the tattoo, etched out in small cursive letters.

She leans in for a closer look. The tattoo reads *a comet appeared* in a tasteful serif typeface. She gives it the barest touch. "When did you get this?"

"When I came to college and read *Roslyn* for the first time. The title poem really stuck with me. It's a love poem to Lydia, of course."

She smiles. "A youthful mistake?"

"Mistake? God, no, I'm mad about it. And I'm being an embarrassing fanboy again, sorry." He rolls his shirtsleeve down and his pale skin disappears fold by fold.

"I'm used to it at this stage." She pauses. "I was looking for a biography of Ben, and there doesn't seem to be one. You'd think he'd have enough fanboys for one decent biography."

"Well, you know why that is."

He says it like it's an inside joke, but she doesn't follow.

"Lydia guards the archives so well that it'd be difficult to write anything meaningful or insightful. And I don't think anyone's been brave enough to even attempt a straight biography since the Conlon-Hayes episode."

That name again. "What happened there?"

He looks past her for a moment, and she gets the impression he's choosing his words carefully. "It's a story among us Crowe scholars. Now, how much of it is true, I don't know. Back in the eighties, Julie Conlon-Hayes wrote a biography of Ben that was supposed to be no-holds-barred. She was friends with your grandparents, so she had great access. By all accounts, they really opened up to her. And there have been suggestions that Conlon-Hayes had an affair with Ben. But then Ben died, and Lydia squashed the project. It was never published."

"Seriously?"

He holds up his hands. "The whole incident could be exaggerated, or misreported, of course. But you can see how it's become a kind of legend among Crowe scholars. This insider's biography, written in the year of Ben's death. The holy grail."

"So, neither Lydia nor Julie has ever confirmed it?"

"Not since Ben's death, no."

"And is Julie still alive?"

He hesitates. "Yes. I've spoken to people who knew her a long time ago. She used to be a brilliant woman. That was before she went off to West Cork to drink herself into oblivion."

Justin starts talking about Julie Conlon-Hayes: how he came upon her work when he first went to university, how her feminist critiques of Swift and Wilde and Synge blew his mind. She lets him talk for a while about Conlon-Hayes's scholarship before steering him back to the subject.

"Did she and Ben really have an affair?"

"According to herself, they did. Some people see it as a cynical attempt to pull Ben's legacy out from under your grandmother. If, as Julie says, he wrote most of *Roslyn* while staying with her in West Cork, then she can claim more insight into the last year of his life than Lydia can."

"And what do you think? Were they actually . . . ?"

He laughs. "Honest answer is, I don't know."

They've been talking for an hour; outside the light is fading.

"Would you like another one?" he asks, his eyes dark as he downs the dregs of his coffee. She ignores the part of her that wants to stay, pulls on her coat, thanks him for the talk, wishes him a happy New Year.

"Are we saying that already?" he asks, smiling.

He offers her his gloved hand as they part. She stares at it, confused, until he laughs self-consciously and pulls her into a hug. He smells of cloves and sweat, and of the cigarettes she tasted on him just weeks before. She suspects this is not just a parting hug, but a final one.

"You seem different."

They are sitting by the fire, reading. Beth catches Lydia watching her over the top of her book. With her face half-hidden, her gaze is sharpened somehow.

"Different how?"

"Unhappy in yourself. You can talk to me, you know. I know all about unhappiness."

This is true, Beth knows; Lydia keeps her grief close, like a favorite shawl she draws around herself for comfort.

"I don't think you listened to my advice," Lydia half-sings.

"What advice?"

"About men. I know a long heartbroken face when I see one."

Beth stares at her book. She's read the same sentence several times over, its meaning refusing to give itself up. "I'll survive."

"That's all we can do, Elizabeth, once we let men into our hearts."

"That's bleak."

"It's the truth! And you deserve better than that, do you hear me? *You* get to decide what happens in your own life. Not some fella."

"What is this—our fourth session now? I hope you're finding it helpful."

"All good so far."

"Well then, let's dive in."

". . ."

"I'm sorry, I retract that. How is swimming going?"

"Good. It feels . . . more on my own terms, now. More manageable."

"Is that important to you? To have things on your own terms?"

"Isn't that important to most people?"

"Some more than others."

"That's something I've learned about myself, I suppose. Commitment, discipline, the ability to give yourself over . . . that's what matters in sport. I thought I had that, but only up to a point."

"Do you remember when it changed for you?"

"When I joined the elite squad, I think. It was ruthless— everyone watching each other, comparing. You couldn't show weakness. I thought I was already operating at a high level but . . . I mean, the logs? The stats, the training plans, the food diaries? I even had these stupid affirmations written on Post-its stuck to my mirror, so I'd see them first thing every morning. *I am a well-oiled machine*, that kind of thing. I don't know, I just felt like . . . like I was constantly monitoring myself, assessing myself, nearly—*spying* on myself. It began to feel horrible."

"Did you talk to anyone about those feelings?"

"No. I didn't feel like there was anyone I *could* talk to. My swimming friends were in the same situation, and I didn't want whatever doubt I was feeling to infect their thinking. My normal friends just didn't get it. My mother has enough to be worrying about. My father . . . It's the whole foundation of our relationship, and I'd have been wrecking it."

"Do you not think that the fact that he's your father is the foundation of your relationship?"

"I know what you're saying. But the way he used to get . . . If I won, he'd be on top of the world for weeks. And if I lost, it'd be like, this gray cloud would descend. I'd nearly be afraid to talk to him. Sometimes I felt like I was responsible for his emotional well-being."

"That's a heavy burden to carry."

"I think . . . I think my grandmother would have given me permission to quit, actually. If I'd spoken to her. I regret not doing that. It would have been better than . . . well."

"So how did you make your needs known? If not by talking to someone?"

"It wasn't very mature."

"I'm not here to judge your levels of maturity, Beth."

"I waited until the most important race of the year. The Open. I was supposed to be going for an Olympic qualifying time. But by then it felt like I was sleepwalking. My heart wasn't in it at all. But I was still determined to go through with it, you know, for everyone else's sake. For my dad. But I didn't even manage that."

"What happened?"

"I stood on the block, but when the signal went, I didn't dive in. I just stood there, rooted to the spot."

Beth makes it back to campus for the new semester before Sadie does. At first she's pleased to have the space to herself, but the tiny flat has no focal point without Sadie; no flicker of projected movies, no annoying invitations to do things. She sits on her single bed and stares out at the deserted street, the bare climbing wall. The darkness and the chill that seemed romantic in December are insidious in January. Eventually, she stirs herself into routine: makes tea, unpacks, puts on *Bury the Boyfriend* as background noise. But the empty feeling persists. She starts foam-rolling her hamstrings just for something to do, but even the whispering grind of the roller against the carpet begins to sound sinister.

Her mother is confused as she answers the phone. "Didn't you just leave?"

"Sorry. I'm . . . I'm just back on campus. It's all weird and quiet."

"Oh yeah? When's Sadie getting back?"

It's a relief to hear her mother's deep, steady voice; Beth can feel her heart rate slowing incrementally as they talk.

"Not sure. I thought she might be back by now. It's a little eerie on my own, actually."

"Ah, sweetheart. It's all those murder programs you watch. Don't be worrying."

"Don't make me quote campus rape stats at you."

There's a silence, presumably as her mother marshals her patience. "Are you lonely, Beth? You know you can always hop on the DART if—"

"No, no. I'm better off here—get back into the routine, and all that." She rolls back onto the bed, tucks her knees up to her chest. She's not sure how this happens, sometimes—how reaching out to her parents can backfire so quickly, bring out the petulant child in her.

"Oh, of course. Any important meets coming up?"

"There's the Intervarsities in March, that's the main one. Will you come to watch?"

"I dunno, love. It depends on how Lydia is. You know yourself."

"You could both come." She tries to remember the last time Lydia came to a meet. Five years ago, maybe? Beth used to love knowing that Lydia was in the bleachers. The desire to perform for her, to impress her, was the greatest motivation she could have. It always baffled Marina, who hated when her family came to watch; who had to throw up in a toilet stall before taking the starting block.

"We'll see." Alice pauses. "I just realized I didn't get much chance to talk to you over Christmas."

"I know what you mean. When it's the three of us, it's— well, it's all about Lydia, isn't it?"

Minding Lydia, fixing Lydia's drinks, checking on Lydia, listening to Lydia's tirades—Beth and her mother have become a skilled team in this regard. Beth is enjoying the intimacy of the phone, the isolation of their talk. She thinks of the pin-drop silence in the auditorium the day Justin played Ben's voice.

"I meant to say. I've been listening to Grandad's poetry recently."

"What's that?" A plummet in her mother's voice, as if she's just dropped into a chair.

"Just, when I'm getting ready to go to bed, I throw on a couple of his recordings. Like a podcast."

Alice clears her throat. "Those recordings—if they're the ones I'm thinking of—are from the year before he died. He recorded a good amount of his back catalog with RTÉ. Your gran can't bear to listen to them. Says he put all his affairs in order behind her back."

For a moment, neither of them speaks. Her mother's breathing is audible.

"It's nice," Beth offers lamely. "Listening to him. He sounds different to what I thought he would."

"You mean he doesn't sound depressed."

"Yeah. He sounds sort of raggedy, like he's been through some stuff, but also like he's smirking a bit."

"I miss his voice," her mother says, simply.

There is another silence.

"It's nice to hear you talk about him," Beth says. "It doesn't happen too often."

"Everybody talks about him, love. It's all so much noise. I figure the biggest favor I can do for him is to keep quiet."

"I'd love if we could talk about him more."

"Why the sudden interest? Oh, let me guess. College isn't school, right? Suddenly it's sort of cool to have a tortured artist in the family?"

Beth says nothing.

"I'm teasing, love. No, you're right. Let's sit down together sometime soon. We'll give Lydia a few extra-strength hot whiskeys and send her off to bed, and then we'll talk."

"You mean that?"

"I do. But don't get your hopes up for tears or drama. Most of my memories of Dad are very happy." She sighs. "It was the aftermath that was the problem. It's not easy to grow up in the wake of a tragedy, you know? You can't put a foot wrong, you really can't."

She finds Sadie's copy of the *Selected Poems* under a pile of overdue library books. She doesn't remember borrowing it, but she must have—or maybe Sadie snuck it onto her desk. She looks again at the cover. *You have his mouth.* It's a girlish mouth, she supposes; swooping Cupid's bow, full lower lip. Ben's scrappy beard, in this photo, masks it somewhat; she wonders if that's why he grew it.

She opens the book to its contents page. All four collections are represented, as well as a section at the back titled "Juvenilia." After the contents, there's a six-page introduction signed "Lydia Blackwood, August 1990." Beth skims it. Lydia writes in the first person, but restricts her discussion to Ben's work and her experience of editing it. One line leaps out in its strangeness: *Many of the poems in Crowe's third collection,* The Lunar Fields, *were drafted in the summer of 1982, when he separated briefly from his wife*—as if Ben's wife was a different person entirely.

She flips through the pages. Most of the poems that she studied in school are from *Roslyn*; there are huge tracts of his work she doesn't know. A poem titled "the lie" from the "Juvenilia" section catches her eye. It looks different on the page to his later work. Lines are scattered, broken with sudden indentations. There are no capitals.

She reads the poem twice through and still doesn't know quite what to make of it. What "the lie" represents is never specified. There is a presence in the poem, a vaguely malevolent young boy who beckons the speaker silently, following him to and from school, staring at him across the kitchen table and even watching him as he sleeps. The speaker repeatedly asks the boy what he wants, but something changes in the poem—the pace quickens—and the speaker begins to simply ignore the boy. The beckoning figure, so malevolent at the beginning of the poem, becomes pathetic and forlorn.

Beth slips the book onto Sadie's shelf, the final line still rumbling around her mind.

i said no more i said no more i said no more

Sadie leaves it to the last minute, arriving back on campus the night before classes are about to start.

"I'm going to have a golden semester," she announces as she humps her wheelie suitcase over the threshold. "No more hangovers. No more sleeping in. No more one-night stands. I'm a new person. Seriously, I'm thinking of changing my name. To Zadie. Do you think people would find that pretentious?"

Beth hasn't spoken to anyone in a few days and feels caught up short. She clears her throat. "Like Zadie Smith?"

"No no, *Xadie*. With an X." She emphasizes the X in the back of her throat.

"You should go for it. Zadie sounds great. Sorry, *Xadie*."

She flops back on her bed. "Although. Does it make me sound like Xena's less impressive sister?"

"Well, now that you've said it."

They exchange stories from their break. Sadie's involved fending off the attentions of her secondary-school boyfriend, Leo. Beth met him briefly when he stayed over the night of the Freshers' Ball: tall, ruddy-faced, ill at ease in his bootcut jeans, chunky runners and Fitbit. Sadie broke up with him soon afterward and proceeded to score boys who were his physical opposite—wiry, tanned city dwellers who wore scarves.

"The problem is I told him I wanted to break up because I didn't want to do long-distance. But now he thinks that whenever I'm in Laois, it's back on."

"So you had to dump him a second time?"

She nods. "I had to spell out that I didn't want to sleep with him ever again."

They go for a reunion drink in the Central Hotel. It feels strange to be drinking somewhere that isn't packed with students in kinetic clusters, roaring at each other over the music. Here, the patrons have good posture and conservative dress; some of them are reading books.

"Very civilized," Sadie says. "It'd be a great place to break up with someone, for example. You *couldn't* make a scene in here."

"Where did you end things with Leo?"

"In his bedroom. Terrible idea. He managed to guilt me into break-up sex with his big puppy-dog face."

"I thought you told him you didn't want to sleep with him ever again."

"That was after. Oh, I'll laugh about it someday."

Beth keeps an eye on the door, half-expecting Justin to walk through at any moment. It feels like the kind of place she might run into him; but then, she thinks she sees him everywhere. He ghosts his way into every crowd. She tells Sadie about the coffee date—a version of it, anyway. Sadie's face contorts as she processes the news.

"He like . . . deliberately sought you out? On his Christmas break?"

"He's a Crowe groupie, remember."

Sadie's laugh is sharp, and Beth wonders if she's crossed a line somehow, by turning their shared crush into someone attainable—even if just for a coffee. But eventually Sadie takes a swig of her pint, folds her arms and looks Beth in the eye.

"For a time I thought I might be the one to shift the face off Justin Kelleher, but now I see that this most holy of duties has fallen to you. Fair fucks, Beth."

She attempts a laugh. "I don't think that'll be happening."

"And here was I thinking you were an innocent. Or a closet-case. But this makes a lot of sense. You're an athlete—of course you're in touch with your physical side, like."

"It's not the same thing. With swimming, it's like I'm—a machine."

Sadie smiles and gestures in a way that says *You're proving my point.*

"It's like I'm on autopilot—my body knows what to do, I don't have to think about it."

"Still sounding an awful lot like sex."

Beth laughs. "There's a difference between being present in your body sports-wise and sex-wise, is what I mean."

Sadie smirks. "If you say so. All I'm saying is you're young and toned and reasonably attractive, in a gloomy brunette way. You should own it."

"I'm not actually hot, though. Not like you."

"What does that mean?"

"You do things, like. With hair and nails."

"I tend to my keratin, yes."

"And like, masques. With a Q."

Sadie finishes her pint, wincing slightly at the last flat mouthful. "Boys don't actually give a shit about that stuff, Beth. That's for my own entertainment."

"I just don't see how it's fun, I guess."

"And I don't see how reading about other people's horrible murders is fun, but that's the great thing about friends. They look the other way."

Chapter Eight

The next weekend she's home, Beth makes a lasagna from scratch, timing it for half six when her mother arrives in from work. She pops garlic bread in the oven, fixes a green salad, and opens a bottle of red. Her mother is the sort of person who needs to be cajoled into relaxation.

When Beth hears the car in the driveway, she lights a couple of candles. Her mother's face crumples when she sees the table already set and Beth worries she's misjudged it, performing this pale imitation of a caring spouse, reminding Alice of what she doesn't have. But then she smiles.

"Did you do all this for me?" There is such simple joy on her face that Beth feels guilty about her ulterior motives. For not doing it more often. "Is your gran joining us?"

"I was trying to coax her down earlier, but . . . she's busy reading, she says. I'll take her up some dinner later."

Beth sees the worry lines slip back into her mother's face.

"It's just more and more often lately," Alice says. "I've been trying to get her to move rooms. Those stairs are too much for her. But she won't hear of it."

"The more you bring it up, the more she'll resist."

"Don't I know it."

They eat quietly for a few minutes, Alice extravagantly praising everything.

"Remember you said we could talk about Grandad?" Beth finally ventures.

"Ah. That's what this is about." Alice folds her arms. Beth feels like a child, transparently angling to get her way. But after a moment Alice picks up her fork again, gestures with it. "Ask away."

At first, Beth's mind goes blank. "What did you and he talk about?" she finally says. "When it was just the two of you?"

Alice thinks about this. "Weirdly enough, I mostly remember the quiet. We were totally comfortable in each other's silences. We'd take long walks along the coast—Greystones to Bray, that was a favorite of his. And he'd tell me the names of things. Birds and trees. The constellations . . . he had strange old folk names for them, you know? The Great Deer. The Slane. You know what that is? It's a tool for cutting turf. He remembered them from his childhood."

"Slane, that's a new one," Beth says. "I've been going through his *Selected Poems* and enjoying all the weird Midlands stuff, but I don't remember that."

"Oh no, he steered clear of all that in his work. The bogs are riddled with poets, he used to say." She takes a sip of wine and then adds, in a higher register, "I'm not used to seeing you drink."

Beth shrugs. "It's just the odd glass."

"The college effect, I suppose." Her mother's tone is light, reasonable, but also serves to put Beth on her guard.

"Tell me more about how it was for you. After."

"After he died?" Alice fingers the base of her glass. "It was awful and scary, as you might imagine. I already knew what suicide was, but suicide wasn't mentioned. I was told Dad had an illness that made him confused, which in turn made him fall into the sea. I didn't connect the dots. For a few years I thought of it as a spell that had been cast on him. Some malevolent force compelled him off the cliff, him begging all the while not to go, not to have to leave me. It was as good a way to cope as any, I suppose."

Beth stalls, not knowing how far to push. "What happened when you figured out it was suicide?"

"Well, I was devastated. I castigated myself for not realizing it sooner—for not having prevented it, even. And I felt stupid and naive, like I was the last person to know." She laces her hands together. "I suppose in recent years I've come back around to the spell theory. It *was* a malevolent force that took him away from us. We'd have a better shot at treating it, these days."

Beth can see how much it costs her to say even this much.

"Losing Dad wasn't the half of it, Beth. I know you love your gran. I love her too, God knows. She was understandably in bits after Dad's death. But she sent everyone away. No one was allowed into her inner sanctum . . . only me. Her intent was to preserve, as she called it, the honor of the family. She didn't want anyone poking around in Dad's memory, and she never spoke publicly about his death. But Beth." Her voice threatens to break, but it holds. "That meant that I became her only confidante. A twelve-year-old. One minute she'd be crying, telling me how lonely she was, saying how no one could ever replace my father. The next minute she'd be in a rage, listing his failures as a husband, saying he wasn't even that good of a poet, that she was the one who made him great. She was drinking too much, you know." Her voice is faint. "It was a crushing closeness we had. Sometimes I think I ran off with your father just to get away from her."

Beth glances reflexively at the ceiling. There are dragging noises, the soft heft of cardboard, Lydia's grunts as she shoves things around. These faint sounds give the house its pulse, reminding her and Alice that they are never alone, not really. She worries for a moment that Lydia has heard every word.

Alice drains her glass. "I made a deal with her. Soon after you were born. She was struggling, then. She'd alienated a lot of her friends. Especially the ones she made through Ben. Your father and I had just separated, so I told her that you and I would come to live with her, as long as she promised not to talk to you about Ben. I didn't want the same thing to happen to you."

Beth takes this in. Her mother's evasiveness all these years, the strange tensions in the house—it all makes better sense. "She's talking about Ben more frequently, now. Have you noticed?"

Alice nods.

"I keep wondering if she's had a change of heart," Beth says. "Whether she'd consider opening up the archives, even."

Her mother smiles faintly. "I doubt that somehow."

*

Beth hopes that when they run into each other again it will be at the pool, where she is at her least self-conscious and most intimidating. It's the one venue where the power balance is tipped in her favor. She finds herself taking a split second longer when she comes up for air; she breathes to the right and the left, on alert. What color togs did he wear? What color cap?

She sees him on a rainy Wednesday as she crosses campus, her swim bag on her back. Justin goes through the swinging library doors and she follows at a distance. She loses him quickly in the stacks and flares with panic; she has no books or pens on her, she can't sit down and make a pretense of studying. Then she hears him, his voice low and slightly scandalized, barely suppressing laughter. She hates hearing that pitch in someone's voice, can never shake the feeling that she is the object of their derision.

She spots him in the languages section chatting with a male colleague. They mirror each other's body language: arms folded, ankles crossed, toes pitched into the carpet. They are either flirting or squaring off, she thinks; it's a fine line with men. She strums the nearest shelf, waits for him to notice her.

"How's it going, Beth?"

She is proud of her reaction: her sudden pivot, like someone pulled out of deep concentration, then a warm smile to acknowledge him.

The colleague nods to Justin and walks away; is she imagining the smirk on his face? Justin steps closer and she leans reflexively against the shelf behind her. One of his rolled-up sleeves has unfurled. She wants to fix it.

"You never told me you were into Old Norse."

"What?"

He nods at the shelf behind her. "Translations. You were browsing them fairly intently."

"Well, yeah. Don't mind any of that new-fangled Norse. The early stuff's much better."

"You're quick, I'll give you that."

He says this instead of laughing, which would have been more gratifying. She feels the flush breach the skin on her face—God, she is so eager to *please* him. She clears her throat. "That's not how banter works, though. You're meant to say something funny back."

"Why don't you just tell me what you're looking for."

The words are brusque but his expression is inviting. Open.

She assumed his office would be in the Arts Block near the library, but it's down the back of campus, toward the pool. She follows him along the narrow footpath, suddenly conscious of the inadequacy of her fleece hoodie, her canvas shoes, against the rain. She wonders why she doesn't own any clothes in grown-up materials, like Jess does: leather and linen and tweed. Even denim would be a step up. She should have let Sadie give her that makeover.

The downpour occupies them sufficiently that they don't feel the need to talk. At one point he gives her a sympathetic look and points to the sky, as if to say *Can you believe this?* He, at least, is wearing the same sturdy wool coat that he had at Christmas. His sensible hair sticks to his forehead.

The office is a shared one, eight workspaces arranged in two neat rows. There's another guy working at his desk down the back of the room, typing furiously and wearing noise-canceling headphones; he raises a hand to acknowledge Justin but otherwise ignores them. Justin's desk, Beth notices, is the least personalized of the eight, somehow both untidy and featureless.

He digs in his desk drawer for several minutes while Beth looks down at his open spiral-bound notebook, scrawled with spider-maps. He gives her a confused look while continuing to rummage. "I could've sworn it was here."

She is surprised by the sharpness of her disappointment.

It had come to her, in the library, to ask if she could see his signed first edition of *Roslyn*. He'd told her about it at Christmas, when they were discussing the best gifts they'd ever received. It suddenly seems very important that she see it, to connect herself closer to Ben, or to Justin—she's not sure which.

"Sorry. Must be at home."

"Are you sure you really own a copy? Or did you just say it to sound impressive?"

He laughs. "Here, I'm bringing my poetry seminar for a drink on Friday. Kennedy's at eight. You could join us if you like? Sadie will be there."

She hesitates. The Varsities are taking place the following week, and there will be eyes on her, the former elite swimmer.

"I've this meet next week—I dunno if I should be in the pub."

"We won't keep you out all night."

She thinks about it. It is too complicated to explain how, in the week before an event, every thought, every action has to be geared toward performance. To be a sportsperson is to live in a bubble; sometimes the divide between her life and others' is negligible, sometimes it's a gulf. But she is always aware of it, whereas those around her—Justin, Sadie, even her mother sometimes—can't see it.

"Maybe just the one," she says.

Moving through the warm damp air of the pub, she scans the room for a group. She expects to see Sadie in a loose crush of chairs, to be able to sit beside her and admire Justin from across a table. But all she sees is Justin, sprawled in a corner seat with an empty glass in front of him, the ghost of a pint of stout still clinging to its edges. When he sees her he smiles, showing the small gap between his teeth, and folds up the newspaper he was reading.

She stows her bag under the table. "Did everyone go home?"

"They went to the Pav. I said I'd wait for you. We could go join them, or have one here if you'd like?"

She pretends to think about it. "Let's have one here."

It's the third time she's been alone with him in a pub or café and she can't quite understand it; he doesn't do this with everyone, surely. But at Christmas he was firm about what he wanted, or didn't want. She's glad he rejected her, she realizes. It's easier to respect him this way. And now she gets to pursue him again. The distance between them feels like an open, pliant possibility. Maybe all she ever really wanted was a crush.

He sets the drinks down on the table, her Coke looking like the offspring of his pint of Guinness.

"Something else may have found its way in there," he says.

"Pepsi?" She brings the glass to her nose: whiskey. "Oh, you shouldn't have. Swim meet next week, remember? My body is a temple right now."

"It's just the one." He is, she is only now realizing, a few drinks in.

She hesitates.

"I'm sorry." He picks up the glass. "I should have got you what you asked for."

"No, it's okay." She takes the drink back, her fingers brushing his, and drinks before she can think better of it. "Thanks."

She sips once for every three sips he takes, not wanting to finish before him. For a while they just sit there, adjusting to the hum of the room, the sudden barks of male laughter.

He eases a pack of cigarettes out of his shirt pocket. "If a drink is bold, a cigarette's probably out of the question, right?"

"Oh, outrageous."

"Feck's sake." He busies himself with the pack, shaking out a cigarette and tapping it sharply off the cardboard lid. She watches his hands, her whole body suffused with warmth. He fiddles with the cigarette between his fingers, all thought of actually going outside to smoke it seemingly forgotten. He catches her eye, holds it.

"What are you reading right now?" It is all she can think of to break the tension.

"I don't really read for pleasure anymore."

"Yeah, me neither."

This makes him laugh for some reason.

"I'm more of a nonfiction person, anyway," she adds.

"Blasphemy."

"Although I did finally pick up Ben's *Selected Poems* recently. Well, really I just read 'the lie' and became terrified and put it away."

"Terrified by the content? Or by the scandalous lack of capitals?"

She wipes a little window in her drink's condensation. "I read it a few times but still don't know what to make of it. The little boy—the one the speaker keeps ignoring—does he represent Ben? Or a version of himself?"

"How much do you know about Ben's family?"

"Not a whole lot."

"Did it ever strike you as strange that a kid in rural Ireland in the forties would be an only child?"

She thinks of her relatives on her father's side, the seemingly endless string of grandaunts and granduncles that Pearse dutifully keeps her updated on: who's "houldin' well," who's on the way out, who was buried last weekend in Mallow. Her father is one of six.

"I guess I never thought about it."

"This is Catholic Ireland, now. Long before birth control."

"I know only children probably weren't the norm, but I mean, it obviously still happened."

Justin nods. "Apparently his mother had six or seven miscarriages. Another two kids died in infancy."

For a moment, Beth's mind rejects the information; it feels too awful and too private. "Jesus," she manages.

"Yeah. Ben was the lone survivor. Did you know that he was named after an older brother who died? So he's not even the original Benjamin Crowe. Who knows what all of that might do to a child."

"Oh my God. Is that the kid in the poem, his dead older brother?"

"That's one possibility."

Beth doesn't know what her great-grandmother looked like. She realizes, with horror, that she doesn't even know her name. All the blood, heartache and sheer force of will she gave to bring life into the world, and already she has been forgotten.

Justin stops playing with his cigarette. He leans forward. "Are you okay?"

She blinks, studies her glass. "I *think* that I want to know everything. But every bit of information is like a rug being pulled out from under me."

He looks stricken. She wonders whether he'll comfort her if she cries.

"The beckoning," she says eventually, clearing her throat. She wishes she had a copy of the poem in front of her, wishes she could remember it exactly. "The kid in the poem—his brother—is always beckoning."

"I know what you're thinking. It's probably too early a poem to play into the suicide narrative, though."

"But it fits. The guilt he must have felt."

A smile sneaks across Justin's face. "Sorry. It's just—like watching a younger version of myself, coming to the poems for the first time, seeing connections everywhere. Falling down the rabbit hole." He studies her. "You know what I'd most like to say to my younger self? Resist the temptation to relate *everything* back to his death. Even when it seems to fit perfectly. Maybe *especially* when it seems to fit perfectly."

"It's hard not to." She sips her drink; it's almost gone.

He is quiet for a moment. "Sometimes I forget how personal this is for you. I know that sounds idiotic. But . . . I feel like I can talk with you. Be really open. Maybe because I already crossed the line. The damage is done."

Emboldened, she reaches out a hand to the soft underside of his arm. She traces the visible *appeared* at the end of his tattoo. His muscles twitch at her touch, like a dreaming animal, but he doesn't pull back. His gaze flits over her face, eyes to mouth.

"I've been thinking about getting the same tattoo," she says. "Or would that be weird?"

His face is very close and at a slight tilt: an invitation. "What are we doing here?"

"Should we get another round, or—"

"That's not what I mean." He is frowning now, the usually restless eyes glazed over.

She thinks through the options quickly. The dorms were out, for obvious reasons. They could be spotted kissing on the street. Too soon for a hotel.

With a self-possession she never knew she had, she says, "Would there be anyone in your office this time of night?"

By the time they get to his building, the front door is locked, and he can't find his key card. "It's not in my wallet," he mumbles. "It's not where it always is."

She crosses her arms, shivering, as he kneels on the pavement and goes through the various compartments of his satchel. "Check your wallet again."

"It must've fallen out at some stage. Maybe I left it at the pub?"

The key card is eventually located in his wallet as Beth shuffles on the footpath to keep warm. Watching him, she feels a complicated mix of tenderness and impatience. She did not anticipate his being this messy.

She is relieved to see that the lights are off in the shared office; his colleagues have gone home. The key card opens this door too. He turns on the overhead fluorescent light, then changes his mind and switches on a couple of desk lamps instead. Beth wonders if she should sit, then remains standing as Justin roots around in the bottom drawer of the file cabinet. He pulls out a bottle of screw-cap Prosecco, which he decants into two white plastic water-cooler cups.

"Office Kris Kindle gift," he explains.

They smile at each other helplessly: the vibe has died. She accepts the drink, its tepidness making the bubbles harsh on her tongue. He opens his laptop and she thinks he's going to put on some music, when suddenly Ben is in the room with

them, clearing his throat, a quirk in his voice as if he's smiling. *So you land yourself at the water's verge . . .*

"Give me your hand." He pulls her close.

"What are you doing?"

"His voice is like music, don't you think? You could nearly
dance to it."

"Oh, is that what we're doing?" They continue to shamble
around the space together. He stumbles occasionally, but his
hand is sure in the small of her back.

"I like the look of you."

"Justin, you're drunk."

"Doesn't make it any less true."

And in that dark sash a comet appeared—

Then they're kissing.

Her skin is always cold to the touch—her amphibious
tendencies, she sometimes thinks—but his is warm. The
heat from his hands pulses through her thin cotton T-shirt.
She lets her hands tug at his sensible hair.

Ben's words unspool around them.

Justin is sleeping in his office chair, his head tipped back.
Beth worries he'll fall over, or stop breathing, but the longer
she watches him the more at ease, even practiced, he seems;
he must have slept here before. For the first time he seems
vulnerable to her, and in sleep he looks young enough to be
her classmate.

They'd kissed and touched for a hazy hour, in a series of
uncomfortable positions that somehow worked beautifully:
up against the file cabinet, on the desk, sitting on his lap in

the office chair. The chair kept gently rotating, unbidden, as they sat in it, making them both laugh. A couple of times Justin fumbled with the top button of his jeans but she gently guided his hands away, genuinely worried about consent, whether he'd remember in the morning. She won't allow him the excuse that he was drunk.

She watches him sleep. She hopes he'll come to, that she'll have a chance to say goodbye properly, but he doesn't stir. She considers writing a note but in the end just leaves, clicking the door softly behind her.

Chapter Nine

When she wakes, she checks her phone. There is an email from Justin to her personal account, time-stamped 3 a.m.

Beth, I'm still reeling from tonight. I hope you hold on to it, despite the drink and the late hour. We have a lot to talk about, I know, and I hope we'll soon get a chance. Thank you for tonight—I've been wanting it for the longest time.

She almost turns the phone off. Is this what love is, she wonders—feeling mortified, but in a good way? She drafts several responses but they are all too coy or juvenile. Lying on her back, phone clutched in her hand, she decides no email at all is preferable to the wrong one.

She begins to view her phone as a loaded weapon. Being separated from it causes her anxiety. As soon as she gets out of the pool on Monday evening, she gropes in her locker for it, hands still damp. There is an email waiting. She reads it in the changing room wrapped in a towel, oblivious to the chatter around her, the slam of locker doors.

Beth, I'd really like to hear from you. Perhaps I misread the situation on Friday night—I'd been drinking, after all—but I thought we were on the same page. I'd love to talk and sort out any misunderstandings. Coffee tomorrow? x

The construction of the message makes her smile: the subclauses, the friendly but cautious tone, the single "x" that she imagines he fretted over. She replies quickly, not to leave him hanging any longer.

She suggests that they meet at Canister & Kettle, a café that she has heard Sadie and Jess raving about. It is long and windowless with a poured-concrete floor. She sees Justin sitting toward the back, making occasional notes on a big sheaf of paper. She wonders if it's for appearances; if pushed, he could say that this is a meeting with a student, nothing more.

He bounds to his feet when he sees her, a little jittery. Kisses her on the cheek and motions for her to sit. For a moment he just gazes at her. "You're wearing a dress," he says finally.

She looks down at herself, as if surprised at this information. The dress was nicked from Sadie's wardrobe, studied from all angles in the mirror before she left the flat. She liked the way it clung to her waist and hips before flaring out, giving her a feminine shape for a change. Now she smooths it over her knees, the pattern looking suddenly mumsy, more like that of a fussy tablecloth than a garment.

"Sorry. I'm just used to seeing you—"

"In sportswear," she finishes. "I know."

"I like sportswear, don't get me wrong."

"We all have our uniforms." He's in his customary black shirt, black jacket, black pants. Mafia henchman or priest, she's not sure which look he's going for.

"Point taken." He runs a hand over the top of his head, flattening his hair into place. "I have to be honest with you, I have a few gaps from the other night."

"You were locked. Maybe I took advantage of you a bit."

He laughs, but there's a strain to it. "I remember us chatting and drinking and kissing. A lot. But then I drifted off at some stage."

"That's pretty much what happened." There's a brightness in her voice, a cajoling. This isn't something she anticipated, having to make things right for him.

"Okay." He laces his fingers around his cup. "I guess I wanted to meet you on neutral ground somewhere because this . . ." His eyes meet hers, briefly. "This is something I'd like to explore further. But I know I'm crossing several lines here, so if you don't feel the same, that's fine. I'll stop sending you embarrassing drunk emails."

"I liked it."

"You didn't respond."

She pauses. "It's just . . . a lot to be dealing with, you know? You're older, you're in a relationship, you're a lecturer."

He smirks. "I wish."

"You're staff, then. Whatever. You teach students."

"But you knew all this before."

"I know. I suppose it just hit me all of a sudden." She is not quite able to put her finger on the source of her discomfort. Maybe it's that their previous encounters could be dismissed as accidents, or isolated incidents at the very least. Aberrations in real life. Emailing each other, though, implies an ongoing attachment. Emails are evidence. This last bit she says out loud.

"You're worried about my girlfriend?"

"I'm worried that *you're* not more worried about your girlfriend."

He flushes. "Katie and I have been together since we were kids. Well, since we were your age, I mean. We've grown up together, pretty much. But we're more like best friends at this stage." He leans a little closer. "And—I'm so curious about you, Beth—I can't stop thinking about you. I don't want to end up wondering, you know?"

Later, she will puzzle over these clichés that she has heard in a dozen rom-coms and wonder how they sounded fresh and new, coming from his mouth.

He hails a taxi and gives the driver an address in Stoneybatter.

The flat is located on a street of low-terraced redbrick houses, above an Italian restaurant. The building is old and the stairwell is steep; he bounds up the steps ahead of her with an air of familiarity. He fumbles with the keys in the door.

"We don't actually live here," he says. "It belongs to Katie's mom. She Airbnbs it out—Katie and I help with the running of it." He turns back, a little sheepish. "No guests booked in tonight, needless to say."

The apartment door opens to a long, narrow room, with a small kitchen at one end and a nondescript living space— leather couch, fake plant—at the other. The lighting is harsh, and everything is happening, finally, too quickly. They smile awkwardly across the distance between them.

"It's okay if you don't want to do this." He sits on the couch; the faux leather squeaks, unused to being sat on. "I mean. This is a mad thing to be doing."

She catches sight of herself in a decorative mirror in the shape of a sunburst at the far end of the room. She looks like a stranger in the dress—not unattractive, but a stranger nonetheless. She intended this, she tells herself. She's here, after all.

"I want this," she says quietly.

He comes toward her and holds her by the waist. They stare into each other. She is backed up against the couch and he folds her down onto it. He is sure in his movements, unapologetic. Not like the tentative boys she's been with, hands shaking as they unwrap the condom. Justin pushes inside her while they're still half-clothed and comes quickly, clamping his grunts down on her shoulder. She thinks suddenly of Cormac, head down and striving as if turning into his final length. The second time is slower, looser, all for her.

He tries to carry her to the bedroom, but they stumble into the coffee table, upsetting the wine. When they make it to the bed, he pulls her close, the heat from his bare skin almost too much. He closes his eyes, begins to doze, but Beth is wide awake, every synapse crackling.

She is alone when she wakes up. She's confused, for a moment, in the studied anonymity of the room: the chrome bedside lamp, the framed *Le Chat Noir* poster, the blue sheets. She gropes the bedside table for her watch, her phone, something with which to orient herself. Nothing there.

Her clothes are in the other room, she realizes. She does something that she's only seen in the movies: she wraps herself in a sheet and tiptoes out. She assumes that Justin has gone home to his girlfriend and expects to find a polite note or nothing at all, but he's stretched on the couch reading his phone.

He lifts his head up to acknowledge her. "Hey, sleepyhead."

"I didn't mean to fall asleep." She smiles; she can't help it. The rush of affection for him is so intense it nearly throws her off balance. This is new. She has wanted him for months, admired his cleverness, craved his guidance and approval. But she's never thought beyond fucking him until now.

"I was just going to take a shower."

Of course, she thinks—he needs to be clean before he goes home. She starts picking up her clothes from the floor. "I'll just be a few minutes," she says.

"Don't you want to join me?"

They wash pressed together with sensible man-toiletries: a bar of soap, Head & Shoulders. She is as sure of her body and his together and all the attendant possibilities as she is sure of herself in the water.

At some point he says, "I have to get home." They towel off quietly, giving each other space in the small steam-filled room. It seems foolish, considering what they'd been doing just hours before. She isn't sure what their mode of speaking should be now. She rubs her hair between her towel-wrapped palms as if trying to spark a fire.

He smiles. "I never see you with dry hair."

They hesitate by the front door. He grasps her firmly by the upper arms and kisses her on the mouth. Not chaste, but not sexual, either. Wanting to prolong the moment, she burrows hard against his chest, one of his shirt buttons pressing into her cheek. He gives a small huff of surprise, but braces her, his chin settling on top of her head.

After a few moments, she opens the door, waits for him expectantly.

"I just need to change the sheets," he says. "You go on ahead."

Beth doesn't sleep well that night, but then she never does the night before a meet. Whenever she manages to doze off, she wakes with a jolt within the hour, always anticipating her alarm. She watches the square glowing numerals of her clock radio change until it's time to get up.

She boards the bus with a dozen other sleepy kids at 5 a.m., shuffling outside the sports complex in the cold air, pulling the drawstrings on their hoodies tight. There is a quiet hum of chat, but Beth keeps to herself. She and Marina wave tiredly but make no effort to speak to one another.

There is enough space on the bus that Beth can claim a double seat. She settles in for the long drive north, her swim bag nestled in the small of her back, and tries to rest her eyes. The lads in the back seats begin to banter, rumbling to life with the bus's engine. She puts on her headphones and flicks through her music library on shuffle, always in search of a better tune. She catches eyes, briefly, with the guy across the aisle—Dermot?—who she hooked up with at a meet a few years ago. He nods solemnly across the aisle at her.

The sun is not yet up when the bus wheezes to a stop at a service station. Like her teammates, Beth has been hydrating like crazy the last few days; they all make use of the bathroom break. Though Beth isn't hungry, she buys a couple of snacks to eat preemptively, taking on energy to be expended later: cashew nuts, a banana, a protein bar. She barely tastes any of it going down. As the road signs change from bilingual to just English, pale light starts to filter through the cloud cover.

Her father has texted to tell her he's coming. Her thumbs hover over the keypad, unwilling to commit to a response. He'll already be on the road; it's too late to tell him not to bother. She just assumed he wouldn't come, and has been looking forward to getting through the event without his scrutiny and support.

She spots Pearse outside the changing rooms. He beams when he sees her, then hands her an energy drink, green as absinthe.

"Who let you back here?" She is only half-kidding.

"Sure I know every official here. How's the form?"

She shrugs.

"Say no more. I know how you get. You need the nerves, Beth." He grasps her shoulder. "The nerves are what fuel you, what make you great. Okay?"

She nods, breathes.

"Listen, I'm not going to annoy you. I'll head back out to the arena now. I just wanted to say good luck. And remember—don't worry about any of your opposition out there. The only thing you're racing is the clock."

He squeezes her shoulder again and leaves her standing there, the nerves crowding in on her now, the swim bag heavier.

She jumps into the pool for a quick warm-up. Crowded as the pool is, the sluice of water is reassuring after the long bus ride. Afterward, she swaddles herself in layers and orders a double espresso in the gallery café that overlooks the pool. She consumes more caffeine than usual on race days—wanting to be on high alert, to embrace the nerves. She sits in the bleachers and soaks in the familiar sounds of a meet: loudspeakers, the beep of the starting signal, bursts of feel-good pop bouncing off the water.

Around her, swimmers sit in clusters: sipping from bottles of lurid sports drinks and fiddling with phones. A few are balancing textbooks on their crossed legs, dragging highlighters across the pages. The back of Beth's neck prickles and she swears she can hear people whispering about her.

She doesn't move until her own race is announced. She knows most of the other girls in her breaststroke heat from meets over the years. She loves the moment just before the race at the blocks, when the tension is almost unbearable and her muscles are coiling themselves for action. She always waits until the last minute before skinning out of her tracksuit. This is the Olympic moment she used to fantasize about—not the opening ceremony, not winning a medal, but waiting at the blocks before a race, ready to wave into the camera when her name is called.

Her toes grip the stippled block. The starting signal beeps

and she dives, hitting the water at just the right angle, nice and clean. She reminds herself to relax, to pull herself through the water smoothly; controlled power, that's the key. She doesn't have to win the heat; she wants to keep some energy in reserve.

She distracts herself with music and chocolate milk and protein bars until it's time for the final. Some swimmers shower after the heat but Beth prefers not to; once she's got wet in the pool, she tries not to displace that second skin.

Beth spots Pearse in the crowd as she walks out poolside a few minutes before the race. He doesn't see her, too busy scanning the program. Beth feels a rush of affection for him; he is doing his best. She suddenly wishes her mother were here, and Lydia too. The best performances of her life have been born of her craving for approval.

She sits in the front row of bleachers with the other swimmers. The boys tend to wear cans before races; the girls mostly prefer shiny colorful earbuds, like little boiled sweets. She is always curious about what other swimmers are listening to as they wait. Once, she downloaded Michael Phelps's prerace playlist, made up of EDM tracks, but it was too intense for her. She tries to keep her music unadorned: minimalist techno or piano solos. She wants her mind as blank as possible.

They are called and all stand up together, swiftly removing their tracksuit tops and hoodies. Beth wheels her arms forward and back as she takes her place at lane 4. Her body feels warm, tingly, ready. She looks to the far wall and not once to her left or right. *They don't matter*, she tells herself. Pearse's mantra: *You're racing yourself. You're racing the clock.*

When she dives, she feels as if she's suspended in the air. She has the sense that the other swimmers are entering the water before her; no harm. She dolphin-kicks, working her core, before surfacing. She feels strong. She feels good. She can taste the win already.

There's a reason she loves meeting Pearse after a win: she can see her emotions reflected in his face. While she tries to play it cool and be modest around the other swimmers, Pearse is lit up with the savage joy of victory.

"You were a powerhouse out there," he says, hugging her. "At your ease. Even the dive!"

"Nice to win. The time could have been better though."

"Beth, that's the best time you've recorded in . . . how long?"

"I should've pushed on."

He grins, shakes his head. "There'll be a time for pushing on. For now, just enjoy the feeling."

She's sitting alone in the bleachers at the end of the day, watching the last of her teammates compete, when the weight of her seat shifts under her. She hears her name, and looks up to see Cormac inching his way toward her along the bench, Marina following close behind.

"Hey hey," says Cormac, grinning at her. "How's the comeback kid?"

She laughs. "You sound like my dad."

"Seriously though. That was some time."

"Yeah," Marina chimes in, "let's just hope the urine sample comes back clear, right?"

Cormac goes red. "Jesus, Marina."

"I'm joking, clearly." Marina grins at Beth. "Seriously, well done. You looked really strong out there."

"I felt strong." She holds Marina's gaze. "And well done to you guys, too." Marina had blown the competition out of the water in her event—as Beth had known she would—and Cormac had come in a respectable third.

"Thanks, Beth." Cormac begins to worry Marina's fingers in his own, and an awkward silence descends.

"So I guess now you guys are gearing up for the Open," Beth says.

Cormac grins. "Yeah. The pressure's on now. You wouldn't be tempted back, no?"

"I'm actually enjoying being a Varsity swimmer. I dunno. Not sure I should mess with that."

"You should come to the invitational, anyway," Cormac says. "In Limerick, a month before the Open? No pressure, just to get our confidence up and our heads right. And the club would love to have you back."

Marina shoots him a look, but he doesn't notice.

"Coach says it's mostly a team-bonding weekend, anyway," Cormac adds. "Should be fun."

"I'll think about it," Beth says.

"Anyway, our bus is heading out soon. I just wanted to say well done." Cormac winks at her. "We'll see you in Limerick, yeah?"

For a moment Beth thinks Marina will stay—she is getting the same bus as Beth, after all—but she stands up to go with Cormac, wanting to say a private goodbye.

"Congrats again," Beth calls after them.

Cormac stops and turns, his head at an angle. "You're looking well, by the way," he says simply.

She thinks of the previous afternoon with Justin. "Oh . . . thanks." She looks to Marina to see if Cormac's comment has bothered her, but she's smiling.

"He's right," says Marina. "You are."

Chapter Ten

Beth can hear a hollow murmur as she ascends the spiral staircase. She knocks on the door before entering. Lydia is sitting in her purple armchair, a barricade of cushions behind her, the laptop resting on her blanketed knees.

"Hiya, Gran."

"Whisht." Lydia beckons her over. A politician's drone emanates from the computer's muffled speakers. Beth reads the video title: *Sen. Matheson quotes Irish poet Benjamin Crowe.* She faintly recognizes the senator's face; Irish-American genes shellacked over with expensive dentistry and suits.

Beth braces herself for a tirade; it takes her a moment to realize that Lydia is, in fact, delighted.

"I thought you hated it when politicians hijacked Ben's work."

"Oh, only when it's some Irish ignoramus quoting from 'Crucible' at the opening of a bloody Aldi."

Beth sits on the bed, immediately unseating a delicately balanced pile of notebooks. They teeter off the mattress one by one. "Sorry."

"Not at all, girl. How are you?"

"Glad to be home." She looks around the room; it's a while since she's been up here. She eyes the stacks of cardboard boxes lined up against one wall. Ben's archives. Before, they were just part of the structure of the room, so orderly they simply blended into the wall. Now they look unstable.

She tries to keep her tone casual. "Would you mind if I had a look at those, sometime?"

"Hang on there now, one second. You look a bit pale to me. Going flat out, are you?"

Beth's mind flashes on the afternoon with Justin; the sickly, luxuriant feeling of going to bed during the day. "Ah yeah. Pool, study, you know yourself."

"And how is your boyfriend?"

Beth startles. "I—don't have a boyfriend."

"Or girlfriend." Her hands gesture impatiently: *Get on with it.* "Whichever it is you have."

"I don't—I'm not sure where you got that idea—"

"I'm not confused, Beth, or psychic, merely observant. I would suggest you wear a scarf, but in this weather?"

Beth's hand goes reflexively to her neck. Her eyes close briefly: Justin's shark's teeth nipping at her skin. "I'll take that under advisement."

"Good woman." Lydia is grinning but does not question Beth further. Her delight is in the catching-out, Beth realizes, not in the information itself.

"So, the boxes . . ." she continues, trying to keep her tone light. "Would you mind if I . . . ?"

"Oh-ho. You won't throw me off the scent that easily."

"I mean, what's your plan for them?"

Lydia's eyes narrow. "What's my *plan* for them? Now that I'm on the way out, you mean?"

"I didn't mean it that way."

"Then why the sudden interest? You haven't taken up with a Crowe enthusiast, have you?"

Beth winces.

"Oh, Beth. Really, now."

"You know yourself. You can't swing a cat at the university . . ."

"Without walloping one in the face? Don't remind me." She folds her hands on top of the blanket. "I always intended to sell them, if you must know. It's the thing to do. But every time I came close, I'd waver. That's all that's left of him now, those boxes. And then I got the notion that I'd catalog them myself, but of course that turned out to be a much bigger job than I realized. And now I'm too old to get my act together one way or another."

"Ah, don't say that."

"Sure I'll be dead soon enough, and then you and your mother can do what you will with them. Sell 'em to some American university."

Beth reaches for something to say. "You'll outlive us all, Gran."

"Don't patronize me." She says it quietly, matter-of-factly; all sharpness gone from her tone.

"I only meant . . ." Beth is unsure of how to finish that sentence.

"You remind me of him sometimes. Your magical thinking. Your passivity." Her voice is even. "It's a weakness. You'd want to watch that. If you think things just have a way of working themselves out, you're in for an awful land."

Beth breathes deeply, trying to curb her rising panic. "I don't think that, Gran."

"God, you're an anxious little thing, aren't you. All ruffled over a few home truths." Her gaze is filled with pity. "You can have a look if you want. Just make sure you put everything back where you found it. And be discreet. I don't want your mother thinking I encouraged you."

Before Beth can think of a response, Lydia heaves herself out of the armchair and makes her way downstairs.

At first she just looks at the pictures. She finds a thick photo album at the top of one of the boxes, an old-fashioned one with acetate pages, containing photographs of Ben from his childhood right up until just before his death. Someone—Lydia, she assumes—has taken great care to arrange the photos chronologically. She flicks through them, watching Ben age rapidly.

Some of the photos she has seen before, but many are new to her: Ben aged six, outside the forge, in short pants and suspenders, with his father. (There are no photographs of his mother.) Ben after winning a scholarship to St. Flannan's in Ennis. Reddish hair, knobbly knees. Ben at the university in a cap and gown. He and Lydia on honeymoon in the Lake District, gorgeous and young. Their wedding a simple registry office affair. He gets noticeably heavier as the years progress; it becomes him. Photos of him crouching next to Alice as a little girl, quite serious, in a school pinafore. Hobnobbing photos, with Heaney and Motion and even Ashbery—there was a stint in New York in the late seventies that she's never heard about.

The contents of the boxes are markered neatly on the lids: LITERARY JOURNALS, CORRESPONDENCE POETS/EDITORS, CORRESPONDENCE FAMILY. There is a box for each poetry collection. Not sure where to begin, she opens the one labeled THE LUNAR FIELDS DRAFTS/PROOFS. It's filled with lined copybooks of the sort that a kid would use in primary school, with an illustration of a round tower on the cover—clearly Ben's notebook of choice. His handwriting is heavy and cramped, difficult to make out. He revised his poems ruthlessly, if the annotated proofs are anything to go by. She opens the *Roslyn* box and recognizes, with a pang, Lydia's handwriting on the proofs. Ben was not alive to mark them up.

A box at the bottom is labeled MISC. Following some instinct, she digs it out. She sifts unsystematically through postcard reproductions of paintings, flyers for lectures and readings, old fountain pens, yellowing receipts, and even some paperwork for a dental procedure that Ben underwent three years before his death.

At the bottom of the box is a thick typewritten manuscript, titled *Sweet Obscurity: The Life and Death of Benjamin Crowe*, by Julie Conlon-Hayes.

This, she removes to her own room.

Later that night, she begins reading. The title is from a poem in *Goldenvale* called "Autumn Elegy": "Litterfall knows / how to perish in sweet obscurity." She makes a mental note to give the poem a closer read later.

The book begins with a short prologue. *In the wake of a*

suicide, there is a temptation to blame oneself, Conlon-Hayes writes. *A common, even natural response is "I could have done something." This is the reaction of those who believe themselves to be fundamentally good people, capable even of heroic acts. But what arrogance it is to suppose that one could convince a highly intelligent and deeply depressed person that life is worth the bother. I don't include myself in this group. I know who I am, and I know the limits of my capabilities. And from the start, I knew that my presence in Benjamin Crowe's life brought nothing but trouble.*

Beth has to stop reading briefly to permit herself an eye-roll. How elegant, she thinks; how clever. In one paragraph, Conlon-Hayes manages to both protest her lack of arrogance while also contriving to make it all about her.

She arranges the manuscript on her quilt and takes a photo, title page up, trying to think of an offhand yet witty caption to send to Justin. He will lose his mind, she thinks, as will Sadie and Jess.

Just before hitting Send, she pauses. Lydia has trusted her with this, she thinks; Lydia asked her to be discreet. She deletes the email she drafted. She will keep the biography to herself, for now.

Can you make it to Stoneybatter this afternoon? She supposes this is Justin's version of a sext. It's only when she receives his message that she realizes they'd never made any further plans to see each other, although she assumed it wasn't a one-night stand. She's not sure where this certainty came from.

The second time is more playful, conspiratorial. They no

longer have the excuse of giving in to passion or curiosity. This is something they are deliberately choosing.

Without ever acknowledging what they're doing, they begin to develop a pattern. Neither of them has class on Tuesday and Thursday afternoons, and there is a window before Beth has to train and Justin goes home to his girlfriend. If the Airbnb isn't occupied, Justin sends a brief, innocuous email: *See you later?* If she gets there first, Beth waits for him in the Italian restaurant underneath the flat, drinking espressos and catching up on coursework. Before they go upstairs to his girlfriend's mother's apartment, Justin always buys something—a cappuccino to go, a pastry. Beth wonders if it's a sort of offering—to the restaurant for facilitating them, or to the universe, to assuage his guilt. If the waiters notice their routine, they never pass comment.

Afterward, in bed, she's always tense. Her instinct is to put her clothes back on, straighten the sheets, erase the evidence of her presence. Justin keeps pulling her back beneath the covers.

"What's your hurry?" He locks his arms around her. His arms are slightly doughy but strong; still, she gauges that she's probably a little stronger, if it ever came to that.

"I keep thinking a tourist is gonna burst through the door." She turns to look at him. "This is . . . grubby, Justin. That's the only word for it."

"Grubby." He nods. "That's fair. Fun though, right?"

At first, his easy intimacy scares her. Accustomed to schedules and discipline, she isn't sure how to adjust to this decadent lazing under sheets. She tries arranging her limbs in sexy configurations, wonders if she should buy fancy underwear to go with her new dresses. One afternoon when she's sure he's asleep she rummages in her plain, functional bra, trying to conjure cleavage from hard muscle. She can feel him smirking against the bare skin of her back.

"Checking yourself out? It's okay. I like that."

She is mortified, caught in the performance of something that is supposed to be effortless. But gradually the self-consciousness lifts. She scratches herself in front of him. She undresses herself clumsily, which, she has discovered, is the only way to undress oneself while wearing tights. She unpeels them in a faint billowing cloud of dust, tiny particles of dirt and skin circulating in the dry bedroom air. He undresses himself in an interchangeable succession of black outfits: jackets, jumpers, jeans, slacks, shirts, socks, shoes.

"Even your underwear is black," she feels compelled to point out. "What's up with that? The black?"

"Well, it's an affectation, of course."

Against her better judgment, she decides to trust it. She lets her guard down. His actions and words indicate that he likes her, so she believes it. She likes the way he talks to the smart speaker as if they're having a genuine exchange of ideas; she likes the way he tries to make her laugh. He even makes her a playlist made up of ethereal-sounding bands she hasn't heard of. She listens to it while walking around campus, floating inside, with a slow, unstoppable smile on her face.

*

Occasionally Justin brings takeaway food or wine, and she knows on those days that he wants more than just physical contact. He'll invite her to sit. These afternoons tend to run over into the evening; she skips training, he texts home that he's delayed.

"Does it bother you that I'm in a relationship?" he asks once, sitting at the far end of the couch, chopsticks in hand. She senses that he's carefully set the situation up: asking her the question while they're both fully clothed, giving her the space to unburden herself, should she wish to.

She tries not to think about Justin's partner, and he tries not to talk about her, though he sometimes accidentally drops a plural into the conversation: *There's an amazing coffee shop around the corner from our house*, or *When we were in Prague.* Flashes of guilt or jealousy cause Beth to pick at this scab occasionally, and she asks tentative questions about Katie, like what she does for a living (tech) or where they met (college). They live in Rialto; *We usually get the Luas in.* She pictures them in a little redbrick cottage with a brightly painted front door, cooking meals and bingeing procedurals and playing Scrabble, or whatever it is couples who've been together a long time do.

"Not really," she replies. "It's sort of a reminder to make the most of this. It might be over soon."

"Should we put a deadline on it?"

"Justin. It's not a college assignment."

"Careful now, or I'll set a maximum word count as well."

They end up finishing the takeaway food in bed.

"You're being very quiet," he says.

"I'm chewing." She is also thinking. Would their connection survive the emotional fallout that would come if he left his partner? She thinks, *I just want this, whatever this is.*

After another glass of wine, she has the courage to ask, "But seriously now. Do you love her?"

"I love her." No fake request for clarification of the "her" in question. "She was my first love. We've been together for years, know each other's families really well—she's supported me through so much. But I'm not *in* love with her."

"I don't see the distinction. Also, that's such a cliché."

"Maybe, but it's an accurate one."

"What's the difference, then?"

"Being *in* love, it's all ego and excitement. The songs have it backward. It's not that you're happy you've found someone, you're happy you've been *chosen*." He pauses; Beth isn't quite sure if he's gathering his thoughts or simply going for dramatic effect. "But then that feeling fades. You still love the person, but you don't feel chosen anymore. You feel obligated."

"But then isn't being in love short-lived by its very nature? If you wanted to keep that kind of love in your life all the time, it's not so much about finding the right person, it's more about constantly re-creating the start of a relationship." As soon as she sounds it out, the truth of it settles on her. "You've done this before."

"The crazy thing is, I haven't." It is, she thinks, the first lie he has told her. "Now, am I allowed to ask questions about your home life? How's it working out with you and Sadie?"

Having braced herself for a question about Lydia, Beth is taken aback. "How do you mean?"

"Well, you're so different." It unnerves her that he has thought about her and Sadie in this manner—weighed them up against each other, compared and contrasted.

"We are, but I think that's what makes it work," she says eventually. "She lets me be a weird recluse, and I don't judge her for being a party monster."

"Is that what she is?"

"She drinks *so much wine*. I didn't realize people were allowed to drink that much wine."

"You sound jealous."

"Oh, I am!" She's jealous of most of the other students, who felt limited by their parents and their small towns, who experience college as liberation. Beth is constrained by her own habits and circadian rhythms. By alarms and stopwatches. By laps.

Beth skips quickly through Julie Conlon-Hayes's account of Ben's early years: how he grew up poor, the sort of poor that was unremarkable in Ireland of the forties and fifties. The deceased older brother Benjamin is mentioned, as a story Ben told in his cups; the author appears not to have done any research beyond that.

She reads on through his scholarships to boarding school—which he hated—and to the university, which he loved. He met Lydia and embarked on a whirlwind romance. She edited his work from the beginning, publishing him in

Red Gate Review and preparing his submissions for other journals and publishers.

Unbeknownst to the young couple, this working arrangement set a precedent for their relationship. In life, as in poetry, Lydia would become used to cleaning up Ben's messes.

With the publication of his first collection, In a Grove, *in 1965, Ben was met with immediate acclaim. It was then that the first cracks began to appear in the marriage. Lydia had always been regarded as the senior partner in the relationship. Older than Ben, stunningly beautiful and a respected academic and editor, she was the one to whom everyone flocked at literary parties. The emergence of Ben as a startling new voice in poetry altered the balance between the couple, and Lydia had to adjust to playing second fiddle to her husband.*

Some sections are painful to read, and Beth has to take frequent breaks, but she perseveres. As long as she's reading about Ben, he's a little more real to her. He exists in her world, at least for a while.

When she talks to Justin, she finds herself slicing her past into consumable little stories, pithy phrases and sweeping statements. Soon, she realizes, they're doing a version of this together in real time: building their own mythology, smoothing over the parts that don't fit.

"That first kiss, in your room," he says. "Good Lord. I don't know how I forced myself to get out of there."

"What was Christmas all about, then?" she asks. "The whole 'let's be friends' thing?"

"I don't know. I thought it was the thing to do. I mean,

I wanted to make sure you were okay, and establish some boundaries. I also desperately wanted to see you."

She places a hand flat on his stomach. "How are those boundaries coming along?"

In idle moments, she'll trace his tattoo—*a comet appeared*—with her fingers, her tongue. Sometimes he'll whisper the lines in her ear.

"It was Ben who brought us together, really," he'll say.

"Do you think so?"

"I do." Eyes level with hers, serious. "I think we're both a little in love with him."

"I suppose we are," she agrees, and kisses him.

Ben relished his new-found fame. He exuded a powerful charisma and, though devoted to Lydia, was never lacking in female attention. He spoke candidly to me about those early, heady days. "I loved Lydia. I never entertained the idea of being with anyone else long term. But yes, I was unfaithful to her, and she knew it without me having to tell her. She could always read me like a book." In retaliation, Lydia also took the occasional lover. The couple eventually came to an accommodation: both could sleep with other parties, as long as they were one-off trysts and didn't lead to an affair. The birth of Alice in 1976 brought about a renewed period of closeness as they sought to build a stable home for their only daughter. For a time, they were very happy.

But Ben's behavior became more and more erratic. He had a ferocious temper, which I was privy to on more than one occasion. When he was in one of his slumps, as he called them, the slightest provocation could set him off. I once witnessed him throw an unopened bottle of wine at the dining-room wall after it was implied, teasingly, that he had drunk too much at a gathering the previous night. During these periods he could also be paranoid, depressed, and blacked out frequently from drinking, waking up in houses at which he had no memory of arriving, by his own admission. Understandably, this brought no small measure of stress to his wife and put considerable strain on their marriage.

The situation was more complex, however, than his simply being an alcoholic. It is the opinion of this author that Benjamin Crowe was an undiagnosed manic depressive. During his periods of "mania" he was a delightful companion: generous, warm, witty, bursting with energy and stories and creativity. The entire manuscript of Roslyn, *his masterwork, was written in one such period of mania the summer before his death. But these positive spells were twinned with periods of depression. It was during one of these depressions that Benjamin Crowe met his end.*

The phrase rattles around her head in the days that follow. *Undiagnosed manic depressive.* The outdated terminology makes it seem even more cruel. Curious, she looks it up: bipolar disorder replaced manic depression in DSM-III, published in 1980. So even at the time that Julie was writing those words, she was out of date.

Because she's afraid to ask Lydia, she asks Justin. "Was Ben ever diagnosed with a mental illness, do you know?"

"Diagnosed? I don't know." They're lying side-by-side with the bedroom window open; an ambulance croons in the distance. "He certainly addresses his depression in the poetry, as you know. Characterizes it as a black wave, rather than the usual black dog. 'Dogs I like,' he used to say. His religious beliefs caused him a great deal of suffering, too. They conflicted with the life he was leading. But a diagnosis—I've no idea." To her surprise, he cuts up laughing. "Why are *you* asking *me* these things? Are the Benjamin Crowe archives not sitting in your very house?"

"But I mean—you've tried to get past Lydia, too. You know what it's like." She flushes, guiltily.

"You should sneak in there. In the dead of night."

"And what? Smuggle out Ben's diaries to you?"

He winces. "That's another Crowe legend—Lydia supposedly burned them all after his death. But the other stuff— the drafts, the correspondence? It'd be great if you could fetch those, thanks."

She socks him over the head with a pillow, and eases herself up into a seated position. It will be time to go soon. What he has said jogs a memory, an image: her grandmother by the sitting-room fire, feeding it reams of paper.

Chapter Eleven

I first met Benjamin Crowe in New York City. It was 1978, and I was at a party thrown by Gabriel Young, an Irish Studies professor at NYU. I must admit I found Gabe's parties rather painful. They tended to be awfully earnest Irish cultural evenings, with boxty and uilleann pipes and sean-nós. On this particular evening the Jameson had run out and I was making the rounds, saying my good-byes. Then Benjamin Crowe arrived and read a couple of poems—not too many, maybe four or five—in those gravelly, deep tones. I remember being quite shocked by his voice—so croaky it sounded mechanical, like there were gears turning in his throat. It shouldn't have worked, not with poems as fine as his. But everyone was rapt. It brought a sort of dignity to the diddly-eye proceedings.

I'd read some Crowe, of course, and seen photos, but the camera didn't quite capture the impact of his physical presence. I couldn't stop staring at him. He was like a bulky schoolboy, all freckles and flyaway hair, and he seemed to know everyone. He greeted people by clapping them on the shoulder with a big meaty hand. He made his way over to a dark-haired woman and though they didn't touch, I knew instantly that they were married by the way Ben held himself—bending his largeness around her, accommodating her.

So this was Lydia, I thought. I knew her by reputation but I'd never met her, either. They were a handsome couple—him large and fair, her small and dark. Lydia caught me staring. She found a gap in the crowds between us and stared right back. I was embarrassed and left quickly. I don't know why I didn't just go over and introduce myself. We had friends in common. But I was intimidated.

Later on I heard the rumors that Ben had a wandering eye. Lydia's fierce stare made more sense then; perhaps she felt that I'd been watching Ben with a bit too much interest. Even afterward, when I was introduced to her properly and we became friends, I never felt able to broach the first evening we saw each other.

"You're quite competitive in bed, you know. Has a man ever told you that before?"

This said after a brief and, to her mind, affectionate grapple; he pinned her wrists and she flipped him over, her strong swimmer's core catching him off guard. She likes to keep him on his toes.

"Never," she replies. "It's amazing I've made it this far, really, without a man's feedback."

"God. You really are Lydia's grandchild, aren't you."

"I love it when you bring up my grandmother in bed. Really puts a girl in the mood."

She gets cabin fever one afternoon, suggests they go for a drink, even just to Walsh's down the street. He stretches on the bed theatrically and grumbles about being comfortable right where he is.

She is stalking the bedroom floor, trying to find her socks. "If you don't wanna be seen with me, just say so."

"We're having an affair, Beth. Not being seen together in public is sort of the point?"

She slumps on the edge of the bed, pulls on her battered Cons. "You'll have to bear with me, I'm new to this."

"And you think I'm not?"

He puts a hand on her spine, runs it all the way down to the small of her back. She shrugs him off.

He groans, falls back onto the mattress. "It's a shame your grandfather isn't around to advise. There's a man who could conduct an affair."

She turns around to stare at him. "Why are you such a dick?" she asks, frankly.

"That was banter!"

He reaches out to her again; he still thinks the situation can be rescued. She stands abruptly, throwing his prone body off balance. She grabs the last of her things and stalks to the apartment door, without looking back.

The flare of her anger dims as she stomps back toward campus: a half-hour walk. The flat in Stoneybatter is a bubble, but until today she thought of it as a place where they could treat each other as equals.

She'd come so close to telling him about the biography, dropping her little gift in his lap. But Justin had his chance with Lydia, and he blew it. *An ambitious little scholarly shit.* It scares Beth, sometimes, the things she's willing to overlook.

It was Ben I got to know first. My book of Willa Cather essays came out that year and I was giving a public lecture. Hardly anyone showed up—the sort of event that writers hear stories about but secretly believe will never happen to them. The sparse crowd, however, made it all that much easier to spot Ben, slouched in the third row, managing to take up about three seats between his coat and his papers and his big self. He came up to me afterward to say how much he enjoyed it, which was typical of his kindness. My first impression of him was one of largesse. Everything about him seemed bountiful.

He asked me to go to lunch with him. We went to a bar on Mac-Dougal Street and he ordered two plates—mac and cheese, pastrami on rye—and kept saying how sensational his meal was, how there was nothing like it in Ireland. I learned then that Lydia was the reason they were in New York—she was researching a book on Edith Wharton and had been given a residency at the Public Library— and Ben was just along for the trip. I told him I'd written extensively on Wharton and that maybe Lydia and I could talk, compare notes. He took his napkin then, daintily dabbed the sides of his mouth. He looked me straight in the eye and said, "I was hoping to keep you all to myself."

Nothing more happened between us that afternoon. I was still trying to figure him out, and he didn't seem to be in any rush, either. He just kept smirking at me across the table with those big sad eyes. It would be weeks before we even kissed, our restraint compounding our desire, the way it always does.

For all his talk of keeping me to himself, I was properly introduced to Lydia soon after. We ran into each other at a performance of The Best Little Whorehouse in Texas. Ben seized me in the bar during the interval and insisted I join the two of them for a drink afterward. I couldn't tell if Lydia remembered me from Gabe's party. She was friendly, if a little distant, but she warmed up as the night went on. Maybe she'd decided I was no real competition. At *the time, I never would have guessed I'd end up as close to her as I did to him.*

Even though she hasn't spoken to Justin in days, she still feels drawn to the Stoneybatter flat. One evening, she goes to the Italian restaurant beneath, telling herself she's not stalking him; she just wants to feel closer to him. She has a book and a notebook to scribble in, orders coffee and cake— just a student unwinding at the end of the day. She forces herself not to look toward the door every time the bell chimes.

The sentences on the page are refusing to thread together. She admits defeat and looks at the internet on her phone instead. The cake is finished; she picks up the loose crumbs with the tines of her fork. It was worth coming, she thinks. Even though he doesn't show, even if he's with Katie or some other lover, right at this moment. There's nothing wrong with following your gut and your desires. This is something she's always known from swimming, but struggles to put into practice on dry land.

She puts her things back in her bag and pays the bill. The sun is still out; the city scrubs up well in the fine weather, hardly able to believe its good fortune. Walking down the street, she passes a display of Easter bunnies in a shop window, already beginning to warp and disfigure in the unseasonal sunshine.

At the pedestrian crossing she presses the button, wraps her arms around herself as she waits. A double-decker bus is stalled in traffic, blocking her view. When it finally crawls on, she sees Justin on the street opposite, waiting to cross. He locks eyes with her, his face lit up.

It is another several seconds before the lights change and they can walk to each other.

"You came looking for me," he says.

"I was just being nostalgic."

"It's okay. I came looking for you too." He wraps her in his arms, lifting her half off the ground.

"People will see," she says in his ear, laughing.

"I know they will, I know." He pulls back, gives her face the barest touch. "Let them look."

Chapter Twelve

As summer approaches, the flat is more and more in demand. On the rare occasions when it is free, it's usually for a brief window between guests, and Justin can't seem to decide between fucking her or tidying up.

When she sees him on campus unexpectedly, she tries not to do anything obvious, but can't help the slowly spreading smile or the hot pulse between her legs. She finds herself thinking *That's mine*.

One Thursday, she arranges to meet him at an art museum on the north side. They wander echoey rooms together, each stopping in front of different artworks. She is keenly aware of Justin's movements: the delicate way he spins on his heels to turn to the next painting; how he diligently leans in to read the information panel before stepping back to take in the piece as a whole. When he goes to the bathroom, she follows him into the cubicle, taking care that no one sees.

Another day they go to the National Museum to visit the bog bodies. Pearse brought her there when she was a kid, and she remembers being fascinated by the specimens, which looked to her like twisted lumps of bark and leather. All are young men, presented in glass cases, creatures from a dark fairy tale. Some have teeth and matted hair; one is just a torso. The next room is full of ancient brooches and metalwork. The lights glint oppressively off the display cases but the objects themselves are beautiful. There's one piece, a small golden boat from a first-century hoard in Donegal, that makes her heart swoop, with its tiny wire oars and smooth hollow cast. It comforts her that they made toys back then—sweet, useless trinkets out of the most precious thing they could find.

They blink their way back into the outside world and go to a small bookshop, where she buys a paperback novel about murderous teenage girls. Justin buys a collection by an American poet and they make their way up George's Street to a pub he likes, full of big windows and light. They read at adjoining tables, facing the same direction: him with a pint in front of him, her with sparkling water and dry-roasted peanuts, both with plausible deniability. It's enough to be able to turn her head and catch a glimpse of him in profile, his earnest reading-face, his splayed hand under the book; she tells herself this, at least.

The year before Ben died, my husband, Jonathan, and I bought a cottage near a small village in West Cork. The house was so old and crumbling that at first, staying there felt more like camping. But I loved it, down to its rotten beams and strange porthole windows and weeds growing out of the wall. It was the first place I'd lived in that felt like mine. Jonathan worked in the city and only came to the house at weekends. It felt liberating, being alone, spending all my spare time painting and patching and trying to tame the sea grass out front before giving up.

As soon as was practical, I invited Ben and his family down for a writing retreat. Ben liked the place immediately—if not the house as such, then its setting. "It's a different quality of water you get here," I remember him saying, inhaling the salt air. "A different bouquet altogether."

Lydia said that it looked like the kind of house with bodies in the attic. I sensed that she was still sizing me up, as I was her. She wasn't particularly happy about being in West Cork for the summer when she could have been in Dublin. She thought I'd coerced Ben into the book, but he'd been the one who insisted that it be written after I half-jokingly suggested it. In retrospect, I think he knew what he was doing. Even if he was not yet intending to die, on some level he knew he should set down a record. The body intuits these things long before we admit them to ourselves.

Almost every day she considers telling him about the biography, and every day she decides against it. Occasionally he'll mention the archives in conversation, and she keeps her responses noncommittal.

"Sometimes I think Lydia knows exactly what she's doing," he says, exasperated. "I mean, she *is* a genius. And the more she hoards the papers—the more mystery she creates around it—the more the myth of Benjamin Crowe grows."

Beth considers this. "But that's a risky tactic. After a while, wouldn't people just stop caring?"

"Hmm, that's a point. A wise point for one so young."

He often makes jokes or remarks about her youth; it was endearing, at first.

"I've never actually *felt* young," she says. "I think it's because I've been competing against grown women since I was thirteen. And I *am* an adult. Sadie still hasn't forgiven me for being two years older than her."

He laughs. "What happened again? You took a year out for swimming?"

"That was the plan—a gap year between school and college for the great Olympic push. Didn't pan out."

"How come?"

It helps that she doesn't have to look him in the eye. Some instinct tells her not to go deep into this with him. "I crashed out of the elite squad. And with all the drama I messed up my exams in the process, so I ended up having to repeat."

She can feel his breath hesitate on the nape of her neck. "Sounds awful."

"Oh, it was. It took me a long time to make friends with swimming again."

"I like that. Make friends."

He once referred to her shoulders as "weapons"; she understood it to be a compliment. Now he traces them with his knuckles and she unfurls. She doesn't even realize how much tension she's holding in her body until he touches her.

That summer, he only emerged at night, when he could drag himself away from the Roslyn *manuscript. It was impossible to talk to him during the day, when he was working; you'd get a few grunts, or at best a quiet request to close the door and go away. But at night, after he'd put Alice to bed, he came alive. Lydia and I would be sitting on the porch, reading or drinking wine or talking, and he'd scoop one of us up and thunder down to the sea to drop us in. He was exhilarated by the work, wrestling to get free of it. Every day he finished a page—or even a couple of lines—he was a little closer to being liberated. And he was effusive. All I had to do was switch the Dictaphone on and ask him to talk about anything—growing up in Tipperary, meeting his wife, his struggles with alcohol—and off he'd go.*

Lydia warmed up to me after a few days. The solitude in West Cork can drive one a little loopy, and we really only had each other for company. One evening she joined me for a swim. I assumed she had a suit on under her clothes, but she stripped down to nothing and walked calmly, confidently into the water. Soon we were going down to the pier in the village with Alice every day, to buy fresh fish for dinner. And talking—talking about everything. She discovered things about the house that not even I was aware of, finding a dusty record player and a box of old LPs in the attic. She dragged them all the way downstairs just so we could dance after dinner. I have a very vivid memory of her and Ben, dancing drunkenly to the Temptations in the kitchen, leaning into each other as though they'd each fall down without the other.

When my husband arrived for the weekend, I almost resented the intrusion. I'd grown so used to the bubble of Alice, Ben, Lydia and me. But Jonathan slipped into the group with ease, the way he did everywhere. That evening, Ben said he was sick of seafood, and cooked burgers on the old brick barbecue. His face pinked up from the heat of the grill and I lingered with him, watching Lydia and Jonathan talking on the deck. Lydia flirted with my husband quite readily, which even at the time made a certain sense. Jonathan was older and had a certain brand of buoyant, can-do charisma. He took care of things. On the face of it, Ben was the more attractive of the two, but Lydia had spent two decades with a tortured genius at that point.

We ate our burgers and drank cheap beer, and Jonathan insisted on making a batch of old-fashioneds—he'd brought the bitters with him specially. Lydia said she'd help him in the kitchen, and twenty minutes later there was still no sign of them. I was cold and wanted to go inside, but Ben stopped me.

"Come here," he said, holding his arms out to me. "Let them go their way."

He had so much authority, that was the thing—even with his schoolboy grin and the breeze tossing his big mop of hair. He dragged me to him, gently. I wanted to respond, but I couldn't, because I was thinking of Lydia and Jonathan inside. This wasn't the scenario I'd envisioned.

I went inside to the empty kitchen. The countertop of abandoned ingredients was smiling back at me. I went upstairs to bed alone. I lay down clutching my stomach as if wounded, as though my guts would spill out if I didn't hold them in place. Sometime before dawn Jonathan crawled in next to me and I pretended to be asleep. I didn't know where in our run-down old house he had been. I couldn't bear to ask. He went back to the city in the morning. When I got up, Lydia was making breakfast and clearing away the liquor bottles from the cocktails that had never materialized. I knew that was her way of apologizing.

Justin is about to order food on his phone when Beth suggests that they go out. She is pushing her luck, she knows, but she wants to see how he responds. A restaurant is unlike a gallery or a bookshop or even a pub—you are stuck there for a fixed amount of time. She knows all this even as she asks.

"It's a gorgeous evening," she points out. "We can stroll into town, take our time."

He is in a mood to indulge her. He tilts his phone to landscape mode, a gesture she now associates with him texting his partner.

The restaurant is on the other side of the river: busy and touristy enough to give the impression of anonymity. Though they have ordered from this place before, Beth has never actually visited the premises and finds it disappointing: low-hanging bulbs with prominent filaments, fake-Eames chairs, earnest electronica pulsing through the speakers. They read the menu, printed on large paper placemats, and order drinks. Justin drums his fingers on the table. "Where the hell are the waiters? Is this an order-at-the-counter situation, or . . . ?"

She places her hand on his wrist, stills it. "Let's just try and relax, okay?"

A waitress finally makes her way over: floral tattoos, a pen stuck effortlessly in her updo, bright red lipstick. She seems to hail simultaneously from the fifties and the future. She turns to Beth. "What can I get for you?"

"Fish tacos, please."

"And I'll have the quesadilla," Justin says.

"I'm sorry, we're all out."

"Seriously?"

"Yes—sorry about that. We've just had a run on them today!"

"I don't understand. It's chicken and cheese between two tortillas. Surely you have those things? In the kitchen?"

The waitress smiles, unruffled.

"Just get the tacos, they're good," Beth says.

"Fine. Two tacos. If it isn't too much trouble." He hands his menu to the waitress.

"Actually, that's your placemat. You just keep that right there." The waitress smooths it out in front of him with passive-aggressive forbearance.

"Thank you," says Justin. "Such elegant table-setting."

The waitress briefly catches eyes with Beth, then moves on to the next table.

Beth stares at him. "Why are you being such a jerk?"

"I'm not. I'm merely standing up for myself as a paying customer."

"So they ran out of quesadillas. You don't have to give the waitress shit about it."

"I *can* if I'm getting bad service."

"She's probably making a tenner an hour."

"I've had to *survive* on the minimum wage—please don't lecture me about it."

She can nearly picture him: working part-time in a café or bookshop while doing his master's, enjoying the martyrdom of working through college. The job would have been a game to him. He was passing through, on to bigger and better things.

She picks up her phone to text her mother, to have something to do with her hands.

"Who are you texting?" he asks irritably.

"Home."

"Oh." He softens a little. "How is Lydia?" he adds, as if dutifully asking after his in-laws.

"Not great, to be honest."

"How so?" He has a habit of this, asking her open-ended questions while looking straight into her eyes. It terrifies her sometimes: the vulnerability she feels, chased by the need to perform.

"She's not herself. Well, I mean she is. She's even more Lydia than usual, in some ways." *But she's rarely unkind.* "Mum thinks her mind's wandering. She's not confused as such, she's just making a lot of odd associations. She compared me to Ben the last time I was home."

"I've been guilty of that myself."

Her shoulders relax a little; they are settling back into their usual warm patter.

"Are you worried about her?" he asks.

She nods. "A bit." She thinks back to the death of her grandfather on Pearse's side when she was eleven. He was remote and kindly; she only saw him a few times a year. In the end, in Pearse's words, he went "downhill very fast," and she wonders if death from old age is always like that, once it starts—you pick up speed as you go. "I asked her what her plan was for the archives, if that's what you're wondering," she adds, harshly. "She says it's up to my mum and me."

"I wasn't thinking that."

She notices a figure coming toward them, but with a halting step, as if having suddenly noticed something is wrong. Beth blanches, then waves half-heartedly.

"Who is it?" Justin's face is pinched.

"Jess."

"Oh, for fuck's sake."

Then Jess is upon them. "Hey, Beth, how's it going?" She looks delighted to see her, compounding Beth's discomfort. Jess turns and looks at Justin, then looks again. "Hi, Justin Kelleher."

Justin responds warmly, and Beth is astonished by the transition.

"I'm just waiting to pick up takeout." Jess leaves a space for them to supply cover stories.

"Hi, yourself," Justin says with just a hint of flirtation. "I'm not sure if Beth told you but she's helping me out with a research paper about Ben Crowe. May as well go straight to the source, right?"

Jess's eyes flit over the table at the conspicuous lack of notes or work materials of any kind. Justin's phone is resting on the table and he grips it reflexively. Beth gropes for words but finds none.

"Ah, okay," says Jess brightly. "I'll leave you to it, so. Beth, coffee tomorrow?"

"Sounds good."

Jess walks away. There is a stillness about Justin; his face remains calm, but in his flitting eyes there's a kind of cold fury.

"Why didn't you say anything?"

"I panicked." She can hear her pulse in her ears. The ice rattles in her water glass when she takes a drink.

"You have to fix this," he says. "You have to sell her a story. Okay? Can you do that?"

She wonders why she ever wanted to be out in public with him. To find out what it was like, she supposes. To be seen with him in front of strangers, to bask in his reflected glamour. Even if they were caught by someone they knew— and there was a part of her that wanted that—she thought it might be a relief. She thought whoever it was would be impressed.

All she feels is embarrassment, and her own smallness.

They sit in silence until their tacos arrive. Beth can barely swallow hers. She feels submerged in a sad solemn feeling, the feeling of wanting to run away from home. But there's a calmness, too: the worst has come, but she's equal to it. She can accommodate it. She was nearly built for it.

Chapter Thirteen

He awoke early on the morning of Sunday 16 November. Without disturbing his family, he took the car and began the long drive south. One witness saw him at a petrol station in Waterford at around 10 a.m. and reported that he seemed calm and in good spirits. He continued his journey to Glanmore in West Cork, where most of Roslyn *was written.*

While staying with me the previous summer, Ben took many walks along the coast to clear his head between writing spells. He knew the terrain well. He parked the car at the village pier and began walking across the fields, climbing over fences as he went. The fields that hugged the coastline ran down to steep cliffs; many were not fenced off.

As expressed in the poem "Autumn Elegy"—in many ways a precursor to Roslyn—*Crowe didn't believe in ashes to ashes and dust to dust, but rather that we come from water and should be to water returned.*

His body was recovered the following day by divers from the Irish Coast Guard, having been washed up on the rocks at the base of the cliff. There were rosary beads in his trouser pocket, but the most gifted poet of his generation did not leave a suicide note.

She goes over the various scenarios as she swims laps the next afternoon. Jess is smart; there's no way she fell for

Justin's excuse, although she also has enough social grace to let him believe that she did.

Beth doesn't want to leave the pool, doesn't want to have to justify herself to Jess. She prolongs her session, following the black rib of tile on the pool's floor, up and down. She thinks of "Dark Vein," her face in the water. *From my mother/ and my mother's mother/ and my mother's mother's mother.*

When she gets to the pub, a tiny wood-paneled room near Stephen's Green, Jess already has a coffee in front of her and is writing in a notebook, despite the raucous chatter from various after-work crowds. She always seems surrounded by her own vacuum of calm.

Beth takes her time unloading herself into the seat opposite: jacket on the back of the chair, bag under the table, headphones zipped into a pocket. "Are you okay for a drink?"

Jess waves her off. At the bar, Beth buys a nonalcoholic beer and decants it into a glass. She sits back down opposite Jess and takes a determined sip.

"Don't look so scared," Jess says. "No judgment here. I mostly want to make sure you're okay."

"Why wouldn't I be?"

Jess chooses her words carefully. "Your—date, meeting, whatever with Justin seemed really uncomfortable. It looked like you were going to cry. I wanted to drag you out of there."

Beth fiddles with her coaster. "How long were you watching us?"

"Long enough." She pauses. "Since when has this been happening?"

"Please don't tell anyone, okay?"

"I won't. Apart from Sadie, obviously."

"Please. Not even her."

"She half-suspects anyway."

Beth reddens. "I thought we were being very discreet."

"Well, I didn't believe Sadie until I saw you two together. There was no way you were just two acquaintances. It looked excruciating."

"You caught us at a bad time. We're not usually like that."

"Not usually," Jess repeats quietly. "So this is a serious thing."

"No. I mean, sort of." She sighs. "I feel for him, okay? I know that makes me an idiot, but I do."

"He's a lecturer, Beth. It's fucked-up behavior—I don't mean *you*, now, just him. It's a massive abuse of power."

"He's a postdoc! Besides, he doesn't teach any of *my* classes."

"Again, no judgment," says Jess, "but are you going to keep seeing him?"

Beth nods, more out of stubbornness than anything else. It would not do if the whole enterprise fell apart under the slightest bit of scrutiny. Maybe, she thinks, there's actually a way that Jess's knowledge can legitimize the relationship. Somebody knows, now; it's more real, more tangible. It exists more fully.

"For the moment, yeah," she says, with a coolness she doesn't feel.

*

On her way back to campus, Beth's phone buzzes dully in her pocket—a text from her mother: *Just FYI, Lydia's going in 4 tests on Thurs. Fairly standard stuff at her age.*

Beth rings back but Alice doesn't pick up. She immediately assumes that her mother is annoyed with her; she hasn't been home for a night in weeks.

She can hear Sadie from the doorway of the apartment, wrestling with a wine bottle. Beth goes into the kitchenette and takes the winged corkscrew from her wordlessly.

"I thought you only bought screw-cap."

"I do. This one was a gift. *Thank* you," Sadie says, as Beth pops out the cork. "It's kind of insane that you're so good at that."

"Just have the knack, I guess." Justin taught her. "I suppose Jess has told you already."

"Told me . . . ? Oh shit. I was right about the Justin thing." She says it lightly, as if she has correctly guessed the twist of an airport thriller and is both pleased and disappointed.

"How did you . . . ?"

"Well, that night we went for drinks after the poetry seminar? Yourself and Justin never showed up to the Pav. And you got in very late that night."

"I see."

"Also I could tell by your mood that you were definitely getting laid, but you never had anyone around, so I figured it wasn't your run-of-the-mill campus romance. Oh, *and* I saw you two on the street together, looking very . . . together."

Beth can feel the heat behind her eyes.

"Ah, Beth." Sadie squeezes her arm. "Don't worry, I'm not mad at you or anything. Sure we joked about it often enough."

Beth nods rapidly. If Sadie saw them, who else did? For the first time, she feels a flutter of fear; the realization that their relationship exists in the world, and the world could intrude at any point, and hurt them. The sensation reminds her of a midrace mistake—a bad dive or turn, a swallow of water. One slip and your time is thrown off, your race beyond recovery. It's impossible to go back and start over; you just have to see it through to the end.

Did you speak to Jess?

Yes. The messages in their long email thread are becoming terse.

You persuaded her there's nothing going on?

Yes. Don't be worrying, everything's fine. X

There is a two-day silence, during which she curses herself for the "X."

When his reply eventually comes, she intuits what it will say before she even opens it.

Beth, I care about you deeply but I think it would be best if we put things on pause for the moment . . . This is risky for us both, and the stress of that takes the good out of what is otherwise an incredible connection . . . I want you to know that regardless of what happens in the future, I'll always be here for you in a friendship capacity . . . I think so very highly of you. You're an extraordinary young woman . . .

There's a spilled-milk feeling in her, a knowledge that things are spiraling out of her control and can't be rearranged to her liking.

In the absence of any contact she stalks him on social media. In his profile picture he is presenting in front of a conference, wearing a lanyard, gesturing; it's clear he uses his channel for professional purposes rather than personal, down to the "opinions are my own" disclaimer. She has to go back to the previous summer to find a photo of Katie.

Katie Bradshaw: she hadn't known his girlfriend's surname until now. It's a beach selfie, both of them grinning into the camera, slightly sunburned, clinking their bottles of beer together. Katie, Beth decides, is a prettier, more polished version of Beth herself, with better hair. There are a couple of solo shots of Katie from the same holiday: smiling into Justin's phone across a dinner table; posing with an elaborate cupcake; wearing a long skirt and sunhat, the sort of seemingly effortless look that Beth could never pull off. *Great few days away with this one!*

She clicks into Katie's profile, but her privacy settings are locked down tight. She checks LinkedIn: Katie is an Account Strategist Executive at a tech firm, "committed to finding optimal solutions for a wide range of clients through both English and German."

Next, Beth looks up the Stoneybatter apartment on Airbnb. Katie is listed as the host, with the same corporate-looking headshot as her LinkedIn profile.

It's just a short series of clicks to book in for the night.

*

Katie sends her a couple of stock cheery messages welcoming her to the flat. It strikes Beth that she uses more exclamation marks than is strictly necessary. They arrange to meet for the exchange of keys outside the flat at lunchtime on the appointed day, a Thursday. Beth shows up too early and goes into the Italian restaurant to wait, texting Katie to let her know. She sits there with her book, not reading, eyes flicking to the door. It feels exactly like waiting for Justin.

The door tinkles and Katie walks in. She is unfairly pretty in person, with the kind of luminosity that implies virtue as well as good genes. She's wearing a loose, floppy sweater and a heavy-looking tote bag on one shoulder, and she is undeniably pregnant. Beth waves to catch her attention. Inside, it feels like parts of her are being discreetly removed.

"Hi, Beth, lovely to meet you. Did you want to finish your coffee, or . . . ?"

Beth shakes her head, trying to get away with saying as little as possible. Katie's accent has traces of American in it; Beth can't tell if she lived there as a child, or if it's just the mid-Atlantic twang of a person who grew up watching *Friends*. The stairway up to the apartment, she already knows, is narrow enough that they'll have to go single file.

Katie shows Beth the contrary lock where you have to jimmy the key; the immersion switch; the gas hob; the cupboard with spare blankets, from which Beth has retrieved clean sheets more than once. Katie gives her the WiFi password, not knowing that Beth's phone already has this information saved, is currently duplicating itself in the cloud on the back of the apartment's broadband. All the while, Beth tries not to stare at her belly.

"So what brings you to Dublin?"

"I'm, um, thinking of going to college here." Even as she says the words, Beth thinks of other potential answers that would have made this simpler.

"Great," says Katie, smiling. "What do you want to study?"

It surprises Beth that she doesn't mention her boyfriend who works at the university. Katie is guarded too, Beth realizes—that, or she doesn't feel the need to make every conversation about her.

"English."

Still nothing. "Ooh, interesting. At undergrad level, or . . . ?"

"Master's," Beth blurts.

"I was thinking, you don't look like a school-leaver. But it's so hard to tell with young ones these days."

"Well, I'm not a young one."

"Of course not!" Katie says, an edge of alarm in her voice. "Sometimes we get guests who are here to scope out the university, but most of them have Mammy and Daddy in tow."

They stand in the kitchen where Beth has eaten half a dozen times and smile awkwardly at each other. The conversation has gone awry without either of them intending it.

Beth asks, "So, when are you due?"

She resolves to ignore him, which would be satisfying if he were messaging her or trying to get her attention in any way. She is tormented on a gut level. She cannot eat, and even more so than usual, is unable to relax. *Stupid girl*, she begins scolding herself, at first internally and then, alarmingly, aloud. A feeling which was once so stabilizing—being seen, being *known*—skitters away from her like dust.

It's not even that she didn't see this coming. When she was alone, in her single dorm bed or in the pool, she knew the likely outcome. But when she was in bed with him, it was easy to construct narratives and solutions, ways that this might all be okay.

Sadie says nothing but has taken to looking at her with sympathy. She gives sudden, unsolicited hugs and starts pointing out the attractive boys that live in the rooms down the hall from them. The idea of kissing someone else makes Beth feel, if not quite sick, then simply exhausted, but this feels too pathetic to admit out loud.

Sadie is becoming a more constant and increasingly sober presence in the apartment. Beth realizes, with a jolt, that it's not just for her sake; exams are looming, and even Sadie is hunkering down to study. Beth finally begins to read the books piled on her desk, now well overdue from the library. She reads the same chapters over and over again, takes frequent breaks to scream into a pillow.

She is sitting reading in the Arts Block—the presence of others always makes her focus more diligently, as if they're looking over her shoulder—when Justin walks by, then stops to read something on the society noticeboards. Her body flares with his proximity. She folds her legs underneath her and hopes he doesn't see her; hopes he will. He walks on, into the windowless depths of the building, and she struggles not to follow.

Then, the week before exams start: *Hey Beth, are you free for a coffee and a chat today? JK.*

She hates the pomposity of the initials. She's not sure how her body can accommodate all the conflicting feelings she has for him.

They arrange to meet in a chain coffee shop in the IFSC, full of harried businesspeople eating factory-tooled sandwiches. His choosing the impersonal venue, a safe distance from campus, seems cruel to her: a warning not to get any ideas. She conjures up memories from their afternoons in the apartment to insulate her against whatever hardship might be coming. He enjoyed the sex at least, that much she knows.

"Hey." He sets his satchel on the table in front of her like a shield. "You want a coffee?"

"I'm okay." She indicates her full cup.

He stands in line for five interminable minutes. Beth keeps rearranging herself. Looking at her phone feels too self-involved; pulling a book from her bag, too self-conscious. In the end she settles for staring out the window at the stream of people until his voice jolts her back inside.

"Sorry about that." He looks good, she grudgingly observes, with a few days' worth of stubble and the beginnings of a tan. She notes with satisfaction the small sweat stains under his arms. "So . . . how've you been?"

She reaches for her coffee cup but it rattles in its saucer, so she leaves it. "Grand. Busy. Exams and all . . . Yourself?"

"I'm okay. The last few weeks haven't been easy." He

leans forward. "I meant what I said, you know. About being friends? And I guess I just wanted to check in and see how you're doing."

"And make sure I'm not going to ruin you. Right?"

He looks exhausted. "Beth. Please. I don't want to fight."

"Were you even going to tell me?"

"Tell you what?"

The terrible finality of what she must do settles on her. She has to strike first. "Katie's pregnant. *Several months* pregnant."

Justin stares at her, hard. Beth is dimly aware of the occupants of nearby tables glancing their way, unable to tamp down their delight at a bit of drama.

"How do you know that?" he finally asks.

"Does it matter?"

"Does it matter," he repeats, shaking his head. "I could ask you the same thing. I mean, is it *really* any business of yours? Have I ever acted as if I was going to leave her?"

"Why didn't you *tell* me, Justin?"

"What would have been the point?"

"Oh, I don't know—honesty? Decency?"

"So we could have had an honest, decent affair, is that it?"

She drops her voice to a hissing whisper. "I didn't know I was cheating with someone whose partner was pregnant." A surge of power goes through her as she says this. She's not used to moral clarity; she feels almost giddy. "All those afternoons we were fucking and she was probably puking her guts up. All those times you texted her to say you'd be late, you were caught at work, you were sorry."

"Stop acting as if you know a thing about my partner. Or care about her. You pursued me, if you recall."

"It was that simple, was it? Poor passive Justin. Couldn't help himself. Seduced by the conniving younger woman. And poor pregnant Katie's too wrecked to have sex with him anyway so what was he supposed to do?"

She stands up in a screech of chair legs. He stands with her, his face conciliatory again, even tender.

"Beth, don't do this. Please, just talk to me. Let's go somewhere quiet . . ."

"There's nothing here, Justin. There's *nothing here*."

Beth takes a sip from the jam jar of wine that Sadie has poured for her. A sticky line of liquid clings to the screw-threads on the jar's mouth; she tries, without success, to lick it clean.

"This is my moral line, for some reason. I will not fuck a pregnant woman's boyfriend."

"You're an example to us all, Crowe."

"This is more about his morals than mine, if that makes sense? He's less attractive to me now. Like, he's cheating on the person who's *literally* carrying his child."

Sadie nods. "It's just not classy, is it?"

"Is it weird to demand higher moral standards from the person you love than from yourself?"

"No, that's not . . ." Sadie pauses. "You love him?"

"Forget I said that." A lump lifts in her throat, rebuking her.

*

An email, then, at 4 a.m. one Tuesday night:

Renting out the flat was a low blow, Beth. I'm surprised at you. I know I have to take some responsibility——I should never have gotten in so deep with someone so young——but I genuinely thought you were mature enough. Instead you engaged in this deeply risky behavior to, what——size up my partner? Tell her about us? At the very least, stand there in her apartment & toy with the possibility? Are you really that manipulative? Should I have seen this coming? Maybe you were only ever going to take what you wanted & then leave. Those vicious, efficient little orgasms of yours.

No, that's not fair. I got myself into this mess. I followed my heart & I suppose my dick. Even my intellect was telling me this was the right thing. But that's what love does, I guess. Makes you sick in the head.

Beth gets through her exams by means of coffee, color-coded flashcards and all-nighters. The dull nausea only dissipates when she's in the water, counting her strokes, focusing on her own breath. Outside of the pool she stews in her own skin, swallows hard. She waits for Sadie to latch on to the gossip of the situation, to tease out the details, but she just listens. As Beth articulates her feelings, she's sometimes uncomfortably aware of how much she sounds like a TV show. All these stories end the same way.

On the last day of exams, she sits on the grass by the cricket pitch with Jess, Sadie and a six-pack of Bavaria. She figures she's done enough to scrape a pass in each module. She eases out her limbs, lets the beer fizz over her tongue and the sun warm her bones.

Her phone buzzes in her pocket. *Justin*, she thinks immediately; but no, it's her mother calling. Alice is a texter; she rarely calls.

"Hi, Mum? Is everything okay?"

"Beth, can you make it home tonight?"

The evening has been designated for a pub crawl, which Beth has been considering flaking out on anyway.

"Sure . . . is everything okay?"

It takes Alice a few moments to reply. "It's your gran. Her test results came back."

Pearse is in the living room when Beth gets home. She isn't surprised to see him: Alice often calls on him in times of crisis, like when the pipes burst a couple of winters back. Pearse knows all the numbers to ring. He makes sure the fridge is stocked and remembers to take the trash out.

He stands up to hug her, and when he speaks, it's in the tender, hushed voice she remembers from when he used to read sad myths to her as a child.

"How are you at all?"

"Grand." She's mostly tired, a little drunk. "So what's the plan?"

His face falters. "How do you mean?"

"What kind of treatment is she going to have?"

"Beth, pet. I'm afraid . . . it's just going to be pain management."

"No, she'll fight it."

"She can't, love. It's too far gone. I'm sorry."

She laughs, high and terrible, startling herself. Pearse puts his arms around her and she presses her face to his shoulder.

"You should go up and see her," he says. "In your own time, of course. She's actually in mighty form, considering."

"I can't. I won't know what to say to her."

"She's still your gran. She's not suddenly a stranger just because she's dying."

She is, though, Beth wants to say. Lydia has always been defined by the act of surviving.

Pearse's awkward pats on her back steady her a little. Beth breaks away from him and blows her nose, rubs her eyes.

"It'll do you good to go up to her," he says. "It'll do *her* good. People at the end of their lives, they like to talk. They offload."

She knows she won't be able to give Lydia what she needs. Lydia will want her to be normal—gossiping about college, discussing books, indulging her rambling stories. But normal doesn't feel possible right now.

Her mother gets up off the edge of the bed, envelops Beth in a hug. "You okay?"

She nods, and Alice leaves quietly. Beth wants to call her back, but reminds herself that Alice has probably been waiting for a break for hours. She smiles at Lydia, who is sitting up in bed, the same way Beth has seen her hundreds of times before. Except now there are prescription bottles on her bedside locker instead of gin.

"Hey, Gran," she says as brightly as she can, taking her mother's place.

"Beth, my dear girl." Somehow, she looks even more like a crotchety old countess than usual. "Tell me a story."

Beth is caught off guard. "I, um . . . what kind of story?"

"Any story! Distract me."

"My . . . exams went okay?"

"You don't know what to say, do you."

She feels like she's floundering in a job interview. "I'm sorry."

"No, I'm sorry for putting you on the spot. Dying makes one a lot less considerate of the feelings of other people."

Beth smiles weakly. "I really am sorry, Gran. And I'm scared. That's why I'm acting like an idiot."

She takes Beth's hand. "It's not a disaster. I'm old, for feck's sake. The disaster would have been if we'd lost you. Don't think I haven't noticed what a rough time you've been having the last few years."

Beth blinks forcefully, but a few tears slip down her face.

"I'll tell you a secret, though," Lydia says. "I'm scared too. But don't tell anyone. I have a fearsome reputation to maintain."

Beth laughs. "I won't tell a soul."

"And if anyone asks, I still hold no truck with that religious nonsense. There'll be no deathbed conversions here."

"Got it."

"Now. Tell me what you want."

"What do you mean?"

Lydia sweeps the room with an expansive hand. "Which of my belongings do you want after I'm gone?"

"Jesus, Gran. I don't know."

"Well, stick a Post-it on anything you're interested in, will you?"

"What, right in front of you?"

"Don't be shy. I'd be more offended if you didn't want anything."

Beth glances to the cardboard wall of boxes. "What will happen to Ben's stuff?"

"Well, that's your mother's inheritance. She can sell the archive to one of the American universities that write to me on a regular basis, or she can donate it to an Irish institution and get a nice tax break. I should have done it myself, of course, but I couldn't bear the thought of ghastly academics onanizing over them."

Despite herself, Beth laughs at that. "Language, Gran."

"Ah now. It's my pancreas that's fecked, not my sense of humor." Her smile falters. "You're not happy, Beth."

"Of course I'm not. What'll I do without you?"

"I mean for a while now. You look like you're not sleeping. Or eating for that matter."

"It's just stupid college stuff." But her eyes flash hot again, tears on the brink.

"If there's one thing I want to make sure of before I shuffle off, it's that my one and only granddaughter is happy and healthy."

"I'm doing okay. Really I am." Then she does start crying.

Lydia stretches out her hand, but can't quite reach her. "Let it all out."

Beth presses the heels of her hands to her eyes. Snorts the

tears and phlegm back inside her. "I'm supposed to be comforting you."

"No, you're meant to be distracting me. What happened?"

"It's really stupid and clichéd."

"Fell for the wrong person?"

Beth nods.

"Older? Taken?"

Beth nods again, miserably. "How did you know?"

"I've been on the other side of that scenario."

Beth flinches.

"Oh, I'm not judging. It's no easier on your side of the fence."

Beth meets her eye. There is a moment when it seems possible she might ask about Julie Conlon-Hayes.

"Don't worry, Beth. You may have lost him, but you'll never be fully gone."

"How do you mean?"

"When they argue," Lydia says, "you'll be there, like a shadow. Every fight they have will be about you."

There are days when Lydia is drowsy and sleeps for hours, drifting in and out of a medicated haze. Other times, there'll be a bolt of lucidity.

"You had a look through the archive," she says one night as Beth keeps vigil.

Beth has been scrolling her phone and nursing a cold cup of tea. She is startled by Lydia's voice. "I did, yes."

"Find anything interesting in there?" For a moment, Lydia's gaze seems as sharp as ever.

"I did. I found Julie Conlon-Hayes's manuscript."

Lydia's hands, resting on the duvet, make a little dismissive flutter. "I had to make sure she didn't publish it. Just remember that it's one person's account, okay?"

"Of course, Gran." Beth swallows. "Why did Ben . . . why did Grandad go to West Cork to die? Why there?"

"I've often wondered that myself. There were perfectly good cliffs right here on his doorstep." She pauses. "Julie was always in a rush. Trying to force the issue. 'Come back to West Cork,' she'd say, over and over. Tormenting us. Well, he did go back, in the end. I woke up, and he was gone with the car. I knew where he was headed. Not what he'd done, but where he'd gone."

Beth squeezes her hand. She both wants and doesn't want Lydia to keep going.

"She got to play the widow, you see. She got to stand on the cliff when they searched for him. Everyone being good to her, bringing her tea, draping blankets over her. All those little kindnesses. It should have been me."

"Had she been trying to get Ben to leave you?"

A cloud passes over Lydia's face, and Beth wishes she could take the words back. Lydia's lips move, as if sizing up different things she might say.

"I will say this for her," Lydia says finally. "I don't think she meant for him to leave me that way. I'm sorry now, love, but I'm tired."

Beth stays with her for a moment, turning the conversation over in her head. Lydia's hand slackens its grip on hers as she gets up to leave.

Chapter Fourteen

Toward the end, Lydia is very much herself. The suggestion that she be moved downstairs is dismissed: "I'll be six feet under soon enough. I'm going to enjoy the elevation while I can."

Soon they're all drawn into the performance. The last few days are a coordinated dance around the bed in the attic: Beth and her mother, with cameos from Pearse, Lydia's GP, the public health nurse, and a palliative care nurse from the local hospice. Her name is Susan and she always gently shepherds Beth to a corner of the room when she's turning Lydia or changing the sheets. Somehow, all that this gesture suggests is more frightening to Beth than actually seeing the realities of end of life. *This will happen to my mother*, she finds herself thinking. *This will happen to my father.*

Her parents begin to speak in hushed voices, as if trying to soothe a dying animal. Lydia herself continues to defiantly give orders: *Pile up them pillows. Scratch the top of my spine. No, lower! What's keeping the tea?* As she weakens, she sloughs off the clipped edges of her university accent, returns to her yearning Cork roots. When her voice loses power and she can no longer speak loudly, Beth finds herself raising her own voice, as if she could lend her some volume.

She has never seen anyone or anything die before, but

when it happens, Beth has no doubt, no moment of denial. It's just her and her mother—Pearse at work, Susan downstairs making a cup of tea after a long night's vigil. Lydia's breaths become long and rattly and Alice glances at Beth, meeting her eye. They do not call for Susan. They both place their hands over Lydia's, huge mounds under the covers, and watch her fade out. It's unmistakable.

"She's with Dad now," says Alice, taking deep, steadying breaths. This rare invocation of Ben feels so momentous that Beth wants it to be real: that Lydia will meet him on the other side, wherever that might be. But because Lydia herself never believed in that sort of thing, Beth finds that she can't, either.

Her mother picks the outfit, while Beth and Pearse tidy the dining room and move the table to the garage; the room is to have a new focal point now. Beth lines the perimeter with all the chairs they own; Pearse contributes another six from his own kitchen. The first visitors—guests? mourners?—arrive and Beth supposes that it is a wake now.

She still hasn't cried. She occupies herself carrying trays and dishes for the academics and poets who stand in tight bands of anecdote and laughter. She stares a little too long at a film director and a former government minister, deep in conversation. Later, in the kitchen, a famous playwright stumbles over his sympathies, gesticulating with a brandy glass. She isn't particularly a fan of any of these people, but nevertheless, there it is: the flaring in her cheeks, the shifting in her stomach that says *I am in the presence of power.*

The days before the funeral are full of small, quiet shocks. Sadie and Jess arrive wearing black, tentatively pushing through the crowds, looking far younger, somehow, than they do on campus. Beth thinks about the care they've shown in being here—texting each other, looking up directions online, coordinating lifts—and starts weeping openly. They're alarmed, but they hug her and tell her they're sorry. It's hard to have a conversation, there, in the sea of handshakes and sympathy. They stay for an hour, pausing to respectfully regard Lydia in her coffin. *I wish I'd met her*, Sadie says, and Beth wishes it too, and rebukes herself for not making it happen.

Later, Beth sees her parents hugging—properly hugging, not the cursory one-armed clasp they give each other on birthdays. They confer often, working the room like TV cops giving each other cover. Her father mixes drinks for Lydia's cousins. He knows where to find the glasses and spoons, the cloves and sugar bowl.

Her mother handles the mourners with an ease and grace that startles Beth. Alice soothes the tearful ones; she lets the awkward shufflers know that their presence is comfort enough. Beth isn't used to seeing her mother interact with the public. She feels proud of her poise. It's only late in the day that it hits her: Alice has been preparing for Lydia to die. She's been quietly in readiness for a long time.

"It was a good death," Beth hears her mother say, over and over. Slight emphasis on *good*, to distinguish it from the other, bad one.

This is Beth's first real death, so she has nothing to compare it to.

Late at night, the singsong gives way to a sudden hush, then a lone voice. Peering into the living room from the kitchen, Beth is aware of a space being cleared, as if for a dance. She can't see who's reciting but she hears the voice: old, female, quavery, dangerously close to Lydia's but for the accent.

It takes her a moment to recognize that what is being recited is "Roslyn." She is holding a stack of clean side plates and a bristling fist of cake forks. She clutches them as she waits out the performance.

The room has become starkly silent. It's not the quiet of attention, that low warm buzz; it's shock.

Mercifully, perhaps reading the room, the speaker performs only the two most famous verses rather than the entire six-page sequence. There is a bit of uncertain clapping afterward, and the shuffle of the crowd redistributing itself into the space. The speaker is swallowed up by the bustle.

"I can't believe she showed her face," says the playwright, gesturing with his fork.

"Who is she?"

"That's Julie," he says. "Your gran would have known her well, at one stage. Your grandad knew her even better."

For a moment she thinks she will drop the stack of plates: thinks of the almighty crash, of the shards scattering across the floor. Startled faces turning toward the source of the noise, then softening to pity. *Do it*, a voice inside her says. Instead she heaves the plates onto the counter.

She walks into the living room and scans the faces there. Stretching on her tiptoes, she gently navigates through the crowd, touching the smalls of people's backs, murmuring *Excuse me*. She is looking for the face she has googled, only aged another twenty years.

"Where did she go?" she begins asking different clutches of people. "The woman who recited the poem, where is she?"

But she gets only smiles and shrugs and shakes of the head.

Beth experiences the funeral as if it's happening at the other end of a long, echoing corridor. There are a few heartfelt speeches in the crematorium before the coffin disappears from view. Alice suggests that they scatter the remains later in the summer, on what would have been Lydia's eightieth birthday.

Beth is astonished by the faint lunacy of her grief. She fills silences with inappropriate laughter; she goes into rooms and forgets what she came for; her hands shake; she cannot sit still. She would have preferred numbness, she thinks.

She isn't sure how to tell people that Lydia has died. It seems too huge to go unmentioned, but too common to make a big fuss about. The death of a grandparent is a natural thing, she tells herself. Some of Beth's peers have none left. But this is different; Lydia was the survivor, the one who lived. Beth writes a dozen status updates trying to convey the gravity of the situation and deletes every one.

Sympathy cards jam the letter slot. They lie around in

stacks on the kitchen worktop until Alice starts filing them in shoeboxes, noting the names of the senders, all the thank-you cards she'll have to write. Eventually, she has to upgrade to a larger, sturdier crate. She seems to thrive on the administration of grief.

Beth is in the kitchen making lunch when she hears a furious tearing sound from the worktop behind her. Alice—her quiet, still mother—is ripping up a letter.

"Who sent that?" Beth asks, though part of her already knows.

"No one you need to bother with" comes the terse reply.

Later, Beth finds the pieces of the letter in the bin when she's tossing out a teabag. Alone in the kitchen, she digs out as many as she can, trying to ignore the slime of congealed cornflakes and yesterday's gravy. The stationery is of good quality. She takes the scraps to her room and, spreading them out on her bed, she begins to jigsaw them together. Her mother's anger has ripped the very writing from the paper in places, making some parts illegible. "Dear Lydia," one piece says; "I'm sorry," another. *Strange*, Beth thinks. Who writes a sympathy note to the deceased?

Putting aside the handwritten parts for now, she focuses on the printed letterhead, piecing it together. What she sees causes a hitch inside, like missing a step on the university cobblestones.

Julie Conlon-Hayes, "Roslyn," Old Sea Road, Glanmore, Co. Cork.

They empty the wardrobe first. Beth finds Alice in the attic with her arms full of Lydia's floral shift dresses. Her First

Lady dresses, Lydia used to call them. The drawers and the wardrobe doors gape. A roll of black trash bags lies coiled on the bed, waiting.

"Give us a hand?"

Beth walks over to the wardrobe. "Are you getting rid of everything? Or would it be okay if I kept a few things?"

"Take whatever you like."

She hunts around until she finds a red houndstooth jacket with black piping that she's always loved; it won't fit her, but she wants it all the same. She pulls one of Lydia's headscarves from a drawer, wraps it around her shoulders and poses, hands on hips.

Alice doesn't laugh. She begins to noisily unfurl one of the bin bags, and Beth can tell, by the way she angles her body away and grows more defiant in her movements, that she is trying not to cry.

Beth decides to occupy Lydia's attic room for the remainder of the summer. She wants to sit at the sturdy desk, where Lydia rattled away at her laptop with typewriter-trained hands, or to open a drawer and inhale the cinnamon perfume she always wore. She wants to be haunted.

Climbing into bed, she thinks about the night Lydia died: she and Alice keeping vigil, listening to her breathing get ragged. Lydia smelled less and less like herself at the end. She started to smell like her old first editions, dusty and ripe.

Unable to sleep, Beth grabs her phone from the bedside table and googles *benjamin crowe lydia blackwood*. It's a habit born of loneliness. Up pops the iconic photograph, the one that makes Beth's throat ache. In it, her grandparents are looking beyond the camera, to the left. Lydia stands straight-backed and wistful, as if on the prow of an emigrant ship. She is young and carelessly beautiful. *Good bones*, as she was fond of saying, touching the backs of her fingers to her cheeks.

Next to her, with an arm slung around her waist, stands Ben: red-haired, snaggle-toothed, portly but able to carry it. He wears a smirk that suggests he would have gone to seed rather well. But he died at forty-three, on a stormy November day in West Cork.

Beth thinks of him as she drifts off to sleep, of the dark waves folding over his head.

Side-by-side at the sink: Alice washing, Beth drying. Beth tries to keep her voice casual.

"So Roslyn is a real place, then?"

Alice smiles faintly, letting the question hang there as if it's rhetorical.

Beth plows on. "Turns out it's Julie Conlon-Hayes's house that Ben was writing about the whole time. I know some English students who're going to be majorly scandalized."

Alice tuts. "What makes you think that's the Roslyn he wrote about?"

"What do you mean?"

"I've an elderly customer who owns a semi-d in Grey-stones called 'Innisfree.' Anyone can name a house 'Roslyn.'"

"This is different."

"How is it different?"

Beth knots her hands in the dish towel. She tries to keep her voice even. "Because she's not just some superfan. Ben had an affair with Julie. That's why you didn't speak to her the day of the funeral."

Alice sighs. "That woman has no discretion and no class. She just couldn't help herself. It mightn't have been so bad, but when she dusted off the party piece?" She looks over, her face softening. "Oh . . . Beth. Don't cry."

She can feel her mother's sudsy, wet hands soaking through the back of her T-shirt. She relaxes, allows herself a few hiccuping sobs.

"I'm sorry," Beth says. "I don't know what's wrong with me."

"I do. I feel it too." Alice pats her back. "Grief is the strangest thing that will ever happen to you."

She writes a letter to Julie Conlon-Hayes. It doesn't say much—*I am Ben and Lydia's granddaughter . . . I would very much like to speak with you . . . here are my contact details*—and she doesn't expect a reply. She takes a picture of the envelope and sends it to Sadie. In response she receives a series of exploding-head emojis.

She keeps waiting to hear from Justin—a card, an email at least—but nothing comes. She constructs elaborate narratives in her head about how he's respecting her boundaries in the wake of their breakup, or how he must think she hates him and never wants to hear from him again. But none of them stands up to scrutiny. A death, surely, supersedes the usual post-breakup rules. She wants his condolences. Even Julie Conlon-Hayes made the effort, she thinks. Cursed by the family for decades, but not only did she send a letter, *she showed up.*

Late one night, Beth opens a bottle of Cork Dry Gin, stashed by Lydia behind the *Encyclopedia Britannica*s. There's no tonic so she drinks it with ice, her computer on her lap, sipping as she careens through the internet. The room is dark save for the glow of the screen and so she has no idea how much she's pouring. She refills the glass three times or more, her brain loosening with each drink. She is unsure if what she's feeling is some higher state, or self-obliteration.

Justin's number rings out when she calls, though to be fair it is 1:34 a.m. She pictures him sleeping as the phone judders on the bedside table, or else holding it grimly, like a grenade, smothering its vibrations until it stops. She wonders if Katie is awake and wondering or blissfully unaware.

The next morning: *Beth, please don't call again. I'm sorry for the angry email I sent, but I've been thinking about when we last met. You were right. This way is better for everyone.*

Then, moments later: *I am so sorry about Lydia.*

Chapter Fifteen

Normally, when something bad happens, she is eager to get back to the pool: to the monotony of laps, to the shutting out of all mental noise, to just being a swimmer and not a person. Flutter kick, whip kick. Backstroke, breaststroke, butterfly, crawl. Follow that dark vein of tile all the way to the end, flip, repeat.

But after Lydia dies, the routine quietly collapses. The structure of her life turns out to be flimsy. She stops going to the pool. Her diet goes to hell.

Then there's a morning when she wakes up early, remembers the Limerick invitational she has committed to, and feels that old tug of the predawn swim. Back when she still thought of herself as a future Olympian, she used to launch herself out of bed to turn off the alarm clock, strategically placed on the other side of the room, shivering in the early-morning chill. Now she makes herself get up and dresses quickly in layers, taking care to close the door softly as she leaves. She'd forgotten how much she loves the empty, waking world.

The sound of the rain on the roof of the sports complex reminds her of trad sessions at Pearse's house, how his restless fingers thrummed on the edge of the bodhrán between tunes. She slips into the empty pool and does her usual warm-up circuit. *Funnel funnel funnel!* He's with her in the pool even when he's not physically there, watching; she applies his standards to herself. Even now she's always, on some level, performing for him.

Beth dozes for most of the bus journey to Limerick. There are a couple of seats separating her from Cormac and Marina, for which she is grateful.

She and her clubmates are staying in a hotel the night before the meet to "maximize the team bonding," as their coach puts it. They cluster around him in the hotel lobby as he hands out key cards. Their coach doesn't make a fuss over her, for which Beth is grateful, but her presence causes an uneasy ripple among her old clubmates. Some smile at her, some ignore her completely, but the worst reaction is the overcompensatory one: *Beth! So great to see you back!*

She's rooming with Marina and they ride the lift together to the fourth floor. Marina's arms are crossed; her small, bulletlike body is suffused with even more tension than usual.

"Oh, for fuck's sake," Marina says, as they open their door. "They couldn't even get us a twin room."

They dump their duffel bags on the floor. Beth sits up on the bed, turns on the TV.

Marina paces, taps at her phone. "I'm going to find Cormac. You want anything from the vending machine?"

Beth hands her coins, flicks buttons on the remote. Each channel seems to be on its own 24-hour cycle: news, golf, shows where wealthy British couples buy a second home in

Málaga. The bland content is soothing, like the sound of drizzle. An hour passes and then Marina is back in the room, arms full of bottles of water and energy drinks.

"Did you and Cormac have fun?"

Marina winces. "Don't be mean."

"I'm not. I like you two together."

Marina spills her burden of bottles onto the duvet. She gives Beth a look. "We didn't have sex if that's what you're thinking. Not a good idea to expend nervous energy before a meet."

"Yeah, it's not like you have any to spare or anything."

By 9 p.m., Beth is in her pajamas and under the covers with her phone. She can hear the rhythmic sloshing of Marina showering in the en-suite. Moments later, her towel-wrapped head peers around the door.

"Will you help me with my arms?"

The air is thick with warm shower fug and depilatory cream. Marina sits on the toilet in her bath towel. Beth pulls the curved spatula across the hard-to-reach spots of Marina's hard, wiry arms, creating smooth tracks.

"Good luck tomorrow," Marina says. "You'll fly it."

Beth shakes her head. "I'm a long way off where I was. Just hoping not to embarrass myself, basically."

"You've done amazing times in this event. Historically, I mean."

"Well, exactly. Historically. In the here and now, I haven't put enough training in." She pats Marina's arms dry with a fluffy hotel towel. "Good luck to you, too. It's all about building confidence, right?"

Marina nods. "If I don't make my time, I may as well not show up at the Open."

They settle into bed quietly, back to back. She is aware, suddenly, of Marina's heat, of a commotion on the other side of the bed. The scratch of sheets, a flurry of limbs.

"What are you doing?"

"Nothing. Go back to sleep."

Beth rolls onto her back. "I wasn't asleep. What are you doing?"

Marina is on her belly, arms flung above her head. Her face is hot with effort. "Practicing."

"What?"

"I'm running through tomorrow's race, okay?"

Beth is quiet for a moment, then picks up her phone. "Go ahead. I'll time you."

Marina frowns for a moment, trying to ascertain if Beth is mocking her. Then: "Okay."

"The signal is about to go off. You're crouched." Beth brings up the stopwatch app on her phone. "Ready? Go!"

And Marina kicks, and pulls her strokes, and brings up her head on each side for a breath. This goes on for two minutes. Marina knows how many strokes she needs to make, how many breaths. When she's finished, she stretches her hand out to the headboard.

"Done!" Beth yells. She shows Marina the screen of her phone. "See the time? You've got this, Marina."

She nods, gasping, wisps of still-damp hair clinging to her face. "I've got this."

*

After the meet, they go back to the hotel and order treat meals—burgers, fish and chips, pizza.

Beth is sitting across from Marina and Cormac. She tries to pitch her hearing so that she can make out their distressed whispers, but she can't quite discern what is being said. She feels sorry for Cormac, who, having recorded a personal best, is trying to mute his sense of achievement.

Watching from the bleachers, still numb from her own disastrous final, Beth found herself rising to her feet as Marina touched the wall for the win, delight and envy intermingling inside her. But when the times flashed up on the Omega board, Marina was a full second off her target time. Beside her, Cormac emitted a small moan. Beth focused on Marina, her face small and pinched within the frame of her swim cap, wearing an uncertain smile, willing the numbers on the board to transmogrify into something better.

It has not been a good day for the team overall. They start drinking, and their collective disappointment gives way to hysteria. Beth has never done shots before, but it seems like an evening for trying new things. She hears herself laughing and it has a desperate edge to it. At some point there is dancing, aggressive and jagged.

Around 2 a.m., she slips away from her teammates' quest to find a residents' bar and cautiously navigates her way to the lift. Her body feels misaligned after the desperate race she put it through: trying to overcome a lack of training through sheer bloody effort, and failing. Now she is alone for the first time all day and instinctively hugs herself. On the fourth floor, it takes about thirty seconds to get her key card in the slot of her door, but she manages it.

Cormac and Marina are lying on the bed, Marina draped over Cormac, sobbing. There are a couple of empty bottles on the bedside table. They are both in their underwear, as if they were going to have sex but gave up.

"Sorry, guys," Beth says, carefully enunciating each word so as not to slur. "I can make myself scarce . . ."

"No, no. This is your room after all." Cormac sits up, and Marina slides heavily off him. To Beth, he mouths *Help me*.

Beth sits on her side of the bed and takes off her shoes. "How're you doing, Marina?"

Marina's face is puffy. "I've been drinking and crying all night but it hasn't helped. I'm just dehydrated now."

"Let's maybe watch some TV, how about that?" Cormac's voice is singsong and a little patronizing. He points the remote and a nineties erotic thriller materializes on the screen. Beth has seen it before but can't remember its name.

They watch the movie. Marina starts to drift off and her head falls on Beth's shoulder. In sleep, she moves closer, throws her arm over Beth's waist.

Beth looks at Cormac over Marina's head. *Is she okay?* she mouths. He shakes his head furiously.

As the movie credits roll, Marina speaks up, quite clearly. "Well, that was a load of shite."

Beth laughs. "Jesus. We thought you were asleep."

"Just for a little while. Spoon me, Cormac."

Cormac obliges, and Marina nuzzles closer to Beth.

"It's ridiculous, you know," says Marina. "The way the three of us carry on."

"How do you mean?" Beth asks.

"You and me, playing pass-the-parcel with Cormac. There's no reason any of us should be left out."

Beth glances at the clock. It's 3:45 a.m. "Okay, Marina. Look, it's been a long day."

Marina is smiling up at her. "Just give it a try." And she kisses her.

Beth is taken by surprise, and doesn't react at first. It takes a moment to register that this is fine; nice, even. It feels nothing like kissing Justin, which is a good thing right now; this is something that's okay to want, okay to have. She kisses Marina back, then looks up. Cormac's eyes are hungry and huge.

"Are we doing this?" he asks, as if he can scarcely believe it. "The three of us?"

Beth reaches out to touch his hair. "Sure. Why not?"

Together, they are more graceful than she could ever have imagined.

She wakes with Cormac's long arm looped around her, Marina's face pressed into her back. She disentangles herself as gently as she can. She never really woke up with Justin this way—bundled together, legs interlocked.

Her scalp tingles with hangover. She finds her underwear on the floor and pulls a clean T-shirt from her bag. Taking her phone into the bathroom with her, she texts Sadie: *Went drinking last night after the meet. In bits.* She doesn't look too bad in the flattering bathroom light; last night's makeup has held fast. The nausea comes on sudden and she just manages to dip her head for the toilet in time. *That was a better dive than yesterday.* She hears the words clearly in her mind as she splutters, as if her hangover is a separate entity, judging her.

She sits on the bathroom floor and wipes her mouth with tissue. Sadie's reply comes through: *Of course you are. You have to build up your fitness! Drinking's no diff from swimming that way.* Then a second text, an afterthought: *How did you get on?*

Fourth :(, Beth types back, her thumbs making small electronic splashes on the screen.

Sadie responds: *Dose.*

Her muted reaction, even boredom, is a balm to Beth. There are people who will not think less of her because of a bad race. There are realms in which swimming doesn't matter.

She wants a shower, but would dearly love to get out of the room before Cormac and Marina wake. Her socks and jeans are in her bag; her runners are somewhere else. She brushes her teeth and scrapes her hair back into a bun, then looks at herself in the mirror: relatively human, she decides.

She pads around the room collecting her hoodie, runners and swim bag. Marina stirs sleepily.

"Beth, what are you doing up? Come back to bed."

She shoves her feet into her Converse, panic in the flutter of her fingers as she laces up. "I've to head, sorry."

"She's running off on us, Cormac. Leaving us the morning after like some sort of cad."

"Ah, Beth." Cormac's voice is gravelly with sleep. "Can you not hang around for a while?"

Beth stands up and looks at them, half-sitting up, watching her: loose, easy, smiling. Even Marina seems able to set aside yesterday's devastation, for the time being at least.

"Sorry, guys. I have somewhere to be." And she cannot deny that it feels good to not offer up any further explanation.

"How did your friends react, when you stepped away?"

"I didn't have any friends on the elite squad. My clubmates, though? They thought I'd gone insane. You're so lucky, people told me. To get the call-up. And I felt guilty then, because I wasn't appreciating it enough, or wasn't doing it justice or whatever. Not just letting myself down but all of them, too. I was afraid, all the time."

"Afraid of what?"

"Of not fulfilling my potential. Of letting my father down, after all the effort he put in."

"And how did he react, when you left the squad?"

"He didn't speak to me for a month."

Back at home, Beth unpacks her overnight bag. She upturns its contents on the bed, making a pile of clothes for the laundry, returning items to their drawers. The top drawer of her dresser contains the taped-together letter that she retrieved, in pieces, from the kitchen bin. She feels a sense of forward momentum, a small flutter of hope.

Downstairs, in the kitchen, she finds Alice making tea. "Any post arrive for me?" she asks.

"No. Are you expecting something?"

The quiet is filled with the self-important huff of the kettle. As it builds to a shriek, Beth feels her heart rate quicken. She leans against the worktop, feels its solidity. Breathes. She cannot stay here, stewing in grief. Life is happening elsewhere; she must go to meet it.

She texts Sadie: *You can drive, right? Are you up to much the next while?*

The response comes quickly. *Up to fuckall. And I'm from the countryside, of course I can drive.*

Can you borrow a car, I mean.

Sadie is typing. *Maybe? What do you have in mind?*

She finds herself repacking the bag, replacing the stale clothes with clean ones. Fistfuls of underwear. Her toiletries bag, too. She is packing for an undetermined length of time. On impulse, she grabs the Conlon-Hayes manuscript, stuffs it into her laptop sleeve.

I want to go to Roslyn. You on for it?

Chapter Sixteen

The train is quiet; she has a four-seat booth to herself. She is traveling through country that she has only ever stopped in briefly—to get ice cream or petrol or to pee—while driving with her father to Cork.

This is the landscape Ben wrote about, she thinks, looking out the window—in his earlier work, at least. The hedges are straggly, the sky white. Strung-together phone poles bisect the fields. Houses huddle down in the landscape. Away from the coast, she feels unmoored. She wonders how the patriarchs do themselves in here.

By the time she arrives in Portlaoise, it's dusk. Sadie is waiting for her in the car park, leaning on the bonnet of a small cherry-red hatchback.

"Heya, girl." Sadie hugs her.

"Nice wheels."

"It's my mam's. Her tipping-around car, she calls it."

Beth settles into the passenger seat. "Are we going straight?"

"I haven't packed yet. How about we go back to my house, get some food, head off in the morning? I'd rather drive in the daylight anyway."

Sadie guides the car down several small country roads. The land is flat and tilled. They don't encounter any other traffic, which is just as well, since the road isn't wide enough for two cars to pass.

"So how much of this land is yours?" Beth asks.

"Most of it." Sadie is trying hard to sound offhand.

Her house is an unpainted concrete fortress. The car in the driveway is a black SUV, designed to intimidate other motorists. Sensor lights blink on as they pick their way to the front door, gravel crunching underfoot.

The house is dark and quiet inside. Sadie switches on lights as she leads Beth to the kitchen-slash-dining room. Large picture windows gape out onto the blackness. Beyond them, Beth supposes, is the countryside.

Beth turns once, carefully, in the middle of the floor, letting her bag flare out in a circle. She doesn't hit anything.

Sadie switches on the low overhead lights over the breakfast bar. "Cheese toasties okay?"

"Lovely."

The quiet of the house is starting to unnerve her. She opens a door off the kitchen to a laundry room, being openly nosy now. Shoe racks bearing football boots and wellies line the walls.

"You have brothers, right? Younger brothers?"

"The twins are off on their holidays."

"And your folks?"

"Mam's taken to the bed. And Dad is at a committee meeting, which I think is code for down the pub."

For a moment, Beth has a crazy idea that this is not Sadie's house at all; that she's squatting here, or house-sitting, or the family that used to live here is buried out the back in the slurry pit.

"Wine?" Sadie asks.

"Sure." Beth closes the door, and makes a mental note to stop binge-watching *Family Annihilator Confidential* and *Never Too Young . . . to Murder!*

They dim the lights and eat the sandwiches with huge bowl-shaped glasses of red wine in front of the TV. Around eleven, the front door slams, seeming to rattle every piece of furniture in the cavernous hallway. *Dad*, Sadie mouths. Quickly, calmly, she moves their glasses and the wine bottle behind a large recliner armchair.

The door opens and for a moment, Sadie's father is outlined in the door frame by the light from the hall. "Sadie?"

"Hi, Dad. How was your meeting?" Sadie's voice is somehow both higher and softer than Beth has ever heard it.

"Fine." He comes into the kitchen and snaps on the light switches. Beth blinks at him in the sudden brightness; he's tall, weather-beaten, not unhandsome. He's wearing a green gilet and wellingtons.

"This is my friend Beth, Dad. Remember I said she was staying with us tonight?"

"Hello," he says gruffly.

Beth waves, and immediately feels foolish.

"We're hoping to go to West Cork for a few days tomorrow, if that's all right."

"Fine," he says again. He crosses the kitchen to the fridge and takes out a can of beer; with every step, Beth notices, his wellingtons deposit mud on the pristine tiles.

"Would it be all right if I take Mam's car, do you think?" Sadie asks.

"Well, *she's* not going to need it."

"Right," says Sadie.

He uncracks his can, takes a long drink, and regards them for a moment. "Well. Have a good night." He heads for the door.

"Night, Dad."

Beth releases a breath she hadn't been aware she was holding. Calmly, Sadie retrieves their wineglasses from behind the chair. She catches Beth staring at her, and juts her chin.

"What?"

They're on their third or fourth episode of a cooking reality show; they're invested now.

"I was so glad you texted me," Sadie says. "I was bored out of my skull. The summers can be fairly slow here."

"I was bored, too," Beth says. "I—I missed you."

Sadie looks thrilled. "Look at you, expressing your feelings!"

Beth laughs, but it's true; grief has made her tender.

"Does Julie know we're coming?" Sadie asks.

Beth shakes her head. "I wrote to her, but got no response. I just hope she doesn't refuse to see us. I'm not sure I could handle that."

"Will you be all right? So soon after Lydia, I mean. And Justin . . . You've had a rough time of it lately, Beth, really."

"It's all my own fault." She reads Sadie's confused look.

"The Justin part, I mean. I went into it knowing it would end badly and guess what, it did."

"That's allowed, though," said Sadie. "You wanted him. It's good to go after the things you want."

Beth says nothing.

"Listen to me. I am going to tell you some things now that will sound ludicrous and even insulting and you won't believe me, but they are true. One." Sadie holds up an emphatic index finger. "There will come a time when you will not be wondering, every minute of every day, what Justin is doing. Two." Another finger. "You will meet someone else. Someone handsome and kind. At first, you mightn't even notice him. Or you might just see him as a vehicle for making Justin jealous. But you will fall for this person despite yourself. Three." A third, wavery ring finger. "At some point, this unhappiness you're feeling?—will start to seem like a very long time ago."

Beth is woken before eight by a loud rapping on the window that makes her sit bolt upright. When she parts the curtains, Sadie is waving at her, red-faced, hair flying in the breeze. A huge black Labrador plants its paws on the windowsill, making Beth take a step back.

"This is Waffles," Sadie says, her voice muffled by the double-glazing. "Come say hi!"

Beth makes a series of sheepish gestures to convey that she's still in pajamas and maybe she'll meet the dog another time. Waffles grins up at her with beady yellow eyes.

She considers showering, but decides she'd rather be

ready to leave as soon as possible. She dresses, makes the bed, repacks her things. The long tiled corridor is lined with closed doors. Beth tries one; it's locked. She stops and listens. The quietness of the countryside strikes her again, as it did the night before, lying in bed. She misses the faint lulling sounds of nearby traffic and sea.

Sadie appears at the end of the corridor in socked feet. "Are you ready to go?"

Beth nods.

"Will you wait in the kitchen for a bit? I'm just going to say goodbye to Mam."

They pass each other in the hallway. Beth looks back at Sadie's face in profile, just before she climbs the stairs. She is gathering herself.

After Sadie leaves the dog in his run with what looks like a week's worth of food, they get on the road.

"Will Waffles be all right without you?" Beth asks, when what she really wants to ask is if Sadie's mother will be okay.

"Oh yeah. Dad's around, sure." Sadie ejects a CD from the stereo. "Here, you're in charge of tunes and GPS. I'll buy the petrol if you buy the snacks."

Beth thumbs through the car's extensive collection of mammy-pop: Adele, Elton, Dido.

"Does your mum know we're borrowing the car?"

"Of course."

"I still feel weird that I didn't say hi to her."

"Don't worry about it. She's a very low-key person."

"In what way?"

Sadie doesn't answer.

"Sadie, if you need to talk about anything, you can. God knows I spend enough time yammering about my family."

"Yeah, but your family is actually interesting." She turns the volume up on "Tiny Dancer," precluding further discussion.

Sadie stops at a filling station on the outskirts of Cork city for petrol, coffee and breakfast rolls. They stand in the forecourt on opposite sides of the car, using the roof as a picnic table.

"So, you've probably gathered you're not the only one with a dysfunctional family." Sadie says this between chews, as if there's been no lapse in the conversation.

"I didn't say you were dysfunctional."

"Well, I'm saying it. Waffles is the most well-adjusted of us all, truth be told." She adds another sachet of ketchup to her roll.

"Was your mum okay this morning? You didn't feel weird about leaving her or . . . ?"

Sadie shakes her head. "She's on her own a lot when I'm at college and Dad's on the farm and the twins are at school. She'll be fine." She pauses. "She's class, actually, when she's up and about. Funny, full of energy. And when I was a kid, she was like that all the time."

They chew quietly for a while. Beth tries to think of something to say, then realizes it would be better not to.

"So yeah," Sadie says eventually, "maybe thinking about your messed-up family makes me feel better about my messed-up family. Does that make sense?"

Beth finishes her roll, balls up the brown paper in her fist. "Perfect sense."

As they drive, Beth talks. She doesn't relate events in order, rather as they come to her: Justin, the biography, Lydia's death. What she omits is as significant as what she includes; she doesn't, for example, mention the night in the hotel with Cormac and Marina. It's easier to talk when they're not facing each other, Sadie frowning a little as she navigates the winding roads on the way to West Cork. They are inter-rupted every so often by the GPS: *In two hundred meters, turn left, then slide right.* Sometimes the voice is British, some-times American, but always female.

They don't speak much for the next hour or so. Beth tracks the dot of their car on her phone screen. The wipers squeak softly. She has never wanted to learn to drive until now, watching Sadie: focused, in control.

At the next fork, keep left.

"Your phone keeps buzzing. Who's texting you?"

Beth quickly switches her phone to silent. At some point yesterday, Marina set up a three-way text conversation with herself and Cormac. The two of them have been sending flirty messages all day, trying to catch Beth in the crossfire. She hasn't responded yet.

"It's just app notifications."

"Bullshit. It's a boy. Not effing Justin?"

"Not effing Justin, no." She puts her phone on the floor by her feet, looks out the window. "It seems they were . . . partner-swapping."

"Who? Where?" Sadie is alarmed.

"Sorry. Julie and her husband and . . . my grandparents."

They go over a pothole. The tree-shaped air freshener hanging from the rearview mirror bobs violently.

"Jesus," says Sadie. "That's got to feel weird."

Beth looks out the window. "There's this bit in the biography where Julie describes a night with Ben. I expected that much, but then she talks about Lydia disappearing with *her* husband, Jonathan, as well."

"Go '*way*." Sadie is thoughtful. "Well, I suppose it was the seventies."

"The eighties, actually."

"You know how it is in this country. Always a decade or so behind the curve." She glances at Beth in the passenger seat. "It must have been a shock to read that. With Lydia so recently gone and all."

"I was actually kind of happy for her, to be honest." Even Beth, having never known her grandfather, had sensed how the negative space of Ben Crowe clung to Lydia all her life. "I always thought of her as this long-suffering wife, this heartbroken widow. But at least she got to have some of her own fun, too."

Beth has brought the reconstructed letter with her, even though at this point she knows Julie's address off by heart. The GPS brings them as far as the Old Sea Road, but then they're on their own. To their right, the land falls away steeply to the sea.

Every so often they reach the end of a driveway and Beth

gets out to look for a sign or wall plaque that might display the word "Roslyn." The gardens are thick with bees, hydrangeas and fuchsia. A middle-aged man on a ride-on mower kills his engine to stare at her until she stops skulking around his front wall.

"Maybe we should ask someone?" Sadie suggests.

Then they come upon a house that just looks right. A weather-worn cottage, whitewashed, with a porch in front and an untended garden. One of the gable ends is painted blue, and a porthole-style window looks out from it like a single unblinking eye. A few crumbling farm buildings are strung out in the fields behind. Beth jumps out: all she can hear is the hush of the sea and the soft sound of something grazing, goats maybe, although she can't actually see any.

Sadie lowers the passenger window and leans across. "What do you reckon?"

"I'm pretty sure this is the place." There's no car in the driveway, no lights on, no sign.

"How do you know?"

"I just do." She lets out a yelp when she finds, attached to the American-style mailbox, a small laminated sticker bearing the name *ROSLYN*. Sadie laughs and claps her hands.

They walk around the house, looking for some signs of occupancy, but all the blinds are pulled.

"This feels a bit trespassy," says Sadie. "Also, I'm starving."

They drive down into the village of Glanmore, the road wrapping itself perilously close to the cliff. Sadie opens her window while Beth tries not to look over the edge.

"God, I love sea air." Sadie takes in a deep breath, filling her lungs. "In Laois, now, you'd be afraid to breathe through your mouth. 'Cause of the methane, like."

Beth doesn't respond.

"I can see why Ben loved this place, in fairness."

They park by the pier and drift through the narrow streets. The village has a pleasant gone-to-seed feel to it. There are some gestures to tourism: a couple of swinging metal B&B signs along the street, a corner shop with plastic buckets and spades hanging in the window. They find a pub that serves crab sandwiches, and eat them with a side of Tayto and glasses of stout. They don't speak until they're finished and dusting the crumbs off their hands.

"We should ask the barman about Julie," Sadie says. "Place as small as this, everyone knows everyone."

Beth glances up. The barman is in his early fifties: solid beer belly, dapper in a waistcoat, wiping the bar down with great vigor. Just looking at his industry makes her feel tired. But Sadie has been driving all day, and Beth knows that she should be the one to ask. She gets to her feet.

"Same again?"

"Yes. Apart from the sandwiches. Thanks."

She takes the opportunity as they're waiting for the stout to settle. "Do you know someone locally called Julie Conlon-Hayes? She lives on Old Sea Road."

He nods. "I know her all right."

"Would she be a regular?"

"She's banned from this establishment, actually."

"How come?"

He gives her a look. "There are only so many ways you can be banned from a pub, miss."

"What'd she do, start a brawl?"

"Worse. Never paid her tab." He starts to methodically add heads to the glasses of Guinness. "Ye Crowe fans?"

Beth follows his line of vision over her shoulder, to where Sadie has pulled out her edition of the *Selected Poems*. "I guess so."

"We get quite a few of ye. You'd be surprised."

"What are people looking for, generally?"

"They want to see the spot where he died. There's no grave, apparently, so the cliff is where people go to pay their respects."

"Yes, I've heard it's very . . . scenic."

He glances at her. "I can give you directions if you like."

She nods. He turns a coaster over, takes a pen from behind his ear and begins to draw.

"So, here's the Old Sea Road—did you come from Cork, ye did? You would've passed the turn-off for yer wan's house on the left. Now, here's the harbor, and here's us." He curves his pen inland, marks the pub with an X. "On the *other* side of the village is the cliff. Beautiful views, very Instagrammable, if you're into that."

"I'll bear that in mind, thanks."

They head out of the village on foot. It's quiet and still enough that they can walk in the middle of the narrow road, confident they'll hear a car's approach and have time to stand in to the grass margin. Sadie is holding the coaster-map tightly, and it strikes Beth that it has a cheap heroism about it, like a coin from a video game.

"According to this it's five or six fields out of the village," says Sadie. "The second one with sheep in it. He even drew a little sheep, look."

The field, when they reach it, is bordered by wooden stakes with coils of barbed wire strung between them. Beth is looking for a gate or a stile when Sadie calls her impatiently—she is pulling apart two strands of wire, leaving a gap wide enough for Beth to slip through. Sadie follows her, unaided. Beyond the barbed wire is an electric fence.

"It's not on," Sadie says.

"How do you—"

In response, Sadie grabs the wire and gives her a look. Beth ducks underneath it and starts to walk down the gradual slope toward the cliff edge. White puffs of sheep look over at them and bleat, but don't approach. A lipstick smear of a sunset appears on the horizon; it's later in the day than Beth realized.

There is another string of barbed wire at the cliff edge, but nothing more.

Beth edges close to the drop, glances down. It's not as sheer as she thought—there's a way down, rudimentary steps and footholds cut into the cliff face. There's a small beach at the bottom, just a spit of sand beyond the rocks. She thinks of Hames's High Places Phenomenon, which they covered in semester 1: how feeling the urge to jump might actually be the brain's way of trying to keep you safe.

"I wonder if there's another way to get to that beach," says Sadie. "Looks good for a dip."

I don't swim in the sea. "I don't swim" is what Beth actually says, but this too feels accurate.

Sadie gestures at the view. "Do you ever think . . . do you think places hold on to memory in a way that we can't? Like, there's an echo of Ben here somewhere, if we could just tune in to it?"

"I dunno, Sades." Beth turns across the harbor and points out the house with the blue gable amid the scrub. "You can see Roslyn from here."

Sadie sits on the grass, is quiet a moment. "You think he did it here to punish Julie?"

"I really don't know, Sadie. I don't know what to think."

Sadie squints up at her. "Are you not getting a sense of the place?"

Beth shrugs. "I mean, it's beautiful. Makes me anxious, though."

She closes her eyes, and tries to put herself in her grandfather's place over thirty years ago. She pictures him barefoot, his toes gripping the earthy edge of the cliff. Crouching, tucking his chin to his chest, pointing his palms to the water. Except it couldn't have happened like that. She sits down next to Sadie.

"I'm sorry. Apparently I'm not very good at communing with spirits." She puts her hands in the grass, rips the blades up by the roots. The tearing sensation calms her.

They sit there talking quietly for another while, but when they get up to go, Beth is glad to put her back to the cliff.

Chapter Seventeen

The room in which she wakes is nautical in theme, the walls papered in hopeful blue stripes. Sadie is flat out in a matching twin bed against the opposite wall, dead to the world. Beth lies on her back a moment, allowing flashes of the previous night to accumulate. They'd gone back to the same pub and proceeded to get drunk, and then to prevail on the barman—the same one who'd directed them to the cliff—for a lock-in. Before throwing them out, he was decent enough to call his neighbor at the dockside B&B to give them a room for the night.

They walk groggily to the car, still parked at the pier. The road leading out of the village has a gentle incline. On the cliff overlooking the bay, holiday homes lean up against each other like books on a shelf. Sadie initially crawls along the road but soon picks up speed.

"There's a local up my arse," she says, glaring into the rearview.

Beth keeps an eye out for the turn-off but finds herself staring down at the Atlantic, how it breaks itself against the rocks but comes back again and again. The sea looks different here than back home: a cool green-blue, almost chemical. At home the seagulls act like they own the place, dive-bombing on barbecue burgers and children's 99s.

Here they seem vulnerable, torn scraps of fabric flapping in the wind like improvised flags of surrender.

Approached from this angle, Roslyn is one of those houses that looks like it has a face—windows for eyes, the porch a gaping mouth.

"There's a car out back now," Sadie says. "A banger."

Beth cranes her neck and sees the old boxy car behind the house, its red paint desaturated by age. Until now, she hadn't realized that she was hoping there'd be nobody home.

"Do you want to go in on your own?" Sadie asks.

Beth shakes her head.

The two of them mount the rickety porch steps together. Sadie presses the doorbell. The sound of footsteps from within; the click of the latch. A woman cracks the door open as far as the security chain allows, shielding herself. For a moment, the three of them just stare at each other.

Julie Conlon-Hayes is younger-looking than Beth expected; younger than the voice at the wake. Beth had pictured a frail old woman like her grandmother, even though she'd once worked out that Julie was twelve years younger than Lydia.

"Yes?" she says, looking from Beth to Sadie and back again. "Are you selling something?"

Beth shakes her head, but cannot think of anything to say.

Julie starts to close the door in their faces.

"Sorry," Beth says, panicking. "Please, if I could just—"

Julie opens the door again; she was only unhooking the security chain. She is tall and silver-haired, dressed in a denim shirt and dark cords. She makes Beth think immediately of a character from a movie whose husband went to war and never came back, and so she had to take over the cattle-ranching.

"What do you want?"

"I'm Beth Crowe," Beth says.

Julie blinks and nods, but otherwise doesn't change her expression of mild annoyance. "You're the granddaughter."

"I wrote to you," Beth says, at the same time as Julie says, "Someone pointed you out to me."

"At the funeral?"

Julie nods. "I would have known you anyway."

Beth takes a deep breath, recalling the one-liners that Lydia used to give any journalist or academic who was brave enough to knock on her door. "I'd like to ask you a few things. I mean, if you'd be happy to talk."

Julie sighs. "I was afraid of that."

But still she steps aside, allows them through the door.

Inside, large windows look out on the sea's stark horizon. The main living space has wooden floors and plush, sand-colored furnishings. An artful piece of driftwood rests on the mantelpiece. Between bookcases, there's a narrow, floor-to-ceiling wine rack, mostly full. In the middle of the room is a full-size snooker table, its green felt barely visible under a mess of books and papers.

"Sit down, please," Julie says. She gestures at the couch, on which a very old, very small white dog is lying. "This is Precious, by the way."

They sit gingerly on either side of her.

"You're a good dog, aren't you," says Sadie conversationally. Precious does not react to being petted.

"Lazy old thing," says Julie. "Doesn't budge from the couch most days. Flatulent, too. Tea?"

"Umm . . . yes, please."

Julie turns to Sadie, towering over her. "Who are *you*?"

"Sadie. Is my name. I'm . . . a friend."

"Sadie what?"

"McLoughlin?" Sadie answers, as if she's not sure herself.

"What kind of friend?"

"The kind with a car."

"Ah. The most useful kind, then."

Julie leaves the room; they hear the clink of delft, the rush of a kettle. Beth and Sadie exchange glances, and Beth tries hard to place herself in the reality of the situation: she is sitting in the same house where her grandfather wrote *Roslyn*. Where he spent his last summer. When Julie eventually returns with a tray, there is a bottle of brandy alongside the teapot.

"I know it's early," says Julie, "but your visit has me a bit shook. Would you have a drop?"

Sadie accepts eagerly, holding out her cup and saucer. "In the tea, please."

Beth shakes her head.

"No? Suit yourself."

Instead of sitting, Julie shuffles vaguely and leans against the furniture, glass in hand, as if they're at a party with indifferent canapés instead of in her living room.

"How is your mother?" Julie asks eventually. "I have

pictures of her somewhere, from, oh—she was just a little thing."

"Did you see her at the funeral?"

"I did. Tried talking to her, but it didn't go too well. There was a bit of 'How dare you,' possibly 'Get out of my sight.' Lydia would just have bellowed 'Fuck off.' Not as classy, maybe, but effective."

There's a silence, into which Sadie whispers "Good dog" to Precious.

"I heard your recitation," Beth says. "I didn't see you, but I heard you."

"You're the spit of her, you know that? You're probably sick of hearing it."

They look at each other.

"Why don't you tell me what brought you down here," says Julie, like a doctor.

Beth doesn't know where to begin. "I wrote to you."

"Indeed. Unusual to get a letter these days. Handwritten, too."

"You didn't respond."

"I've been trying. But now look, here you are." She pauses. "Does your mother know you're here?"

"No."

"She thinks she's with me in Laois," says Sadie. "On holidays. In the Midlands! Imagine."

Julie laughs at that. "Ben never much liked the Midlands either, but I think it has its charms." She stops circling and lowers herself into a wicker armchair.

Beth is overheated, but doesn't feel comfortable enough

to start shedding layers. Julie is staring at her as if at a ghost. Everyone seems to be waiting for Beth to speak. She can hear her own pulse.

"It was a shock, hearing about your grandmother's death," Julie eventually says. "I found out online."

Beth can see her, late at night: glass of wine at her elbow, the screen illuminating the lines in her face. Did she see it on Twitter, or on one of the news sites? Maybe she was just checking RIP.ie.

Julie clears her throat. "Did you get my letter of condolence? Or of apology, rather."

"Yes. My mother tore it up."

Julie laughs—not out of deflection, but as if amused and mildly scandalized.

"That's how I came across your address," Beth adds. "I assumed that this was the 'Roslyn' of the poem. But Mum said you named the house *after* Ben's book came out."

"The house is called after the book, that's true, not the other way around. Ben wrote most of it here, did you know that?"

"I read your manuscript. The biography. Lydia kept it with Ben's papers."

"Did she?" Julie sounds more curious than shocked. "Ben named the place, really. 'Roslyn' was his word for joy, for refuge. It's not a place exactly, or not *just* a place. It's a feeling tied to a place. Roslyn existed in this house. It's what we made here."

A feeling of dread in Beth's belly. "You and him."

"Yes, and Lydia too."

It comes into Beth's mind, then, a fragment, hurriedly read: *I couldn't shake the feeling that we were both, at that moment, thinking of the other; that flirting with each other's husbands was just another way for us to connect.* Even when Julie was angry, even when she was feeling sorry for herself, it was always there in the biography, underneath it all. Love.

"What Ben didn't understand," Julie says, "was that he really was the best of us. Without him to hold it all together . . ." She makes a gesture that conveys a small explosion.

Beth speaks slowly. "Are you saying that you and Lydia . . . were close?"

"We were lovers, dear. And Ben knew about it, and even encouraged it. But whatever we had did not survive Ben's death. It didn't even really survive the summer. You see, Lydia had a more vivid sense than I did of how unwell Ben was. And I think she decided that our arrangement here—which I believed to be happy and fruitful for all of us—was unhealthy for him. That it was unsustainable. So they went back home, and we stopped seeing each other."

Beth knows, somehow, that Julie is telling the truth. She shifts in her seat, trying to process her discomfort, or at least put it on pause, to deal with later. "None of that is in your book. You write about being with Ben, but not with Lydia."

"Well, it was in the book originally. I sent the relevant pages to Lydia. I still didn't properly understand how painful the whole subject was for her. She sent the pages back to me, and wrote me a furious letter. I tried to please her then, in rewrites—I cut out our relationship entirely. Wrote carefully around it. I suppose that is the version you read." She pauses, drinks. "It didn't make a difference. Her next letter made it clear that she had no intention of letting me publish any sort of book about Ben. She said she'd sue me for any number of things. And, fatally, she even withdrew her permission to quote from Ben's poems. Without that, I couldn't publish anything."

Beth, trying to process this, has withdrawn into herself. There is a long silence. Eventually Sadie speaks up. "Do you understand, now, why Lydia was so hostile?"

"I think I do. She had a theory—which I think may be at least partly correct—that Ben saw our relationship, Lydia and me, as something that could sustain the two of us after he was gone. A sort of landing place. I don't imagine he ever said it in so many words to her, but he left her with that impression in the weeks before his death."

Beth is near tears now. "You think she thought he died so that the two of you could be together?"

"Goodness, no. Ben died because he could no longer bear to go on living. It was coming for a considerable time and he fought it as long and as best he could. What I'm saying— what Lydia believed—is that the idea of she and I looking after each other made it easier for him to actually end his own life."

They stare at each other. Julie is the first to glance downward. All Beth can hear is Sadie's exhaled breath, as though held in for a long time. Beth thinks of Lydia's introduction to the *Selected Poems*, the strange detached way she wrote about Ben's marriage, as if she weren't a party to it. Had it always been that way?

"Anyway, I think Lydia's old-fashioned morality kicked in once Ben was gone," Julie says. "She could never quite shake off her Catholic upbringing. She was even-handed and permissive when it came to others, but rarely toward herself."

"She shunned you."

Julie nods. "From her perspective, it would not have been ethical for the two of us to have gone on together. It would not have been *proper* for us to be happy. We didn't deserve it after what happened to Ben."

Julie, visibly sagging, suggests that they take a break.

"How about we walk Precious?" Sadie says.

Julie looks doubtful. "You can try."

Sadie stays behind to leash up the dog while Beth goes outside for some air. She kicks stones around the front yard and looks at her phone. There is a text from Alice, and several messages from Cormac and Marina. She doesn't respond.

Sadie emerges from the house, practically dragging the dog behind her. "She's invited us back for dinner."

Beth watches Precious sliding serenely across the gravel, not resisting, but not doing anything to help her own forward momentum either. "Should we just put her in the car?"

"Yeah, let's," Sadie says, scooping up the dog. "I miss Waffles dreadfully all of a sudden."

They drive back to the same pub as the night before for bowls of chowder. Despite—or perhaps because of—the hangover, they are both ravenous. The dog recommences her nap under the table. Sadie is uncharacteristically quiet, not meeting Beth's eye.

When they return for dinner, Julie's demeanor is different. She opens the door with a smile, wearing a complicated sort of top, all twists and jewel tones. There's minimalist piano music playing and a bottle of wine open on the coffee table. Julie pours them all a glass.

"To Ben and Lydia," she says, "and to fresh starts."

She's prepared this time, Beth realizes. She has built a fortress out of her hospitality.

Julie goes off to tend to the meaty smells in the kitchen while Beth sits on the couch next to Precious. Sadie begins poking around in Julie's possessions: sifting through the papers on the pool table, browsing the bookshelves. She embraces the floor-to-ceiling wine rack, rubbing her face against the sealed corks.

Beth laughs. "Stop it, Sades."

Julie sweeps back into the room, holding a tray. "Hors d'oeuvres," she says grandly, setting down a platter of bread, cheese and hummus. She sits down this time, settling back into an armchair, the folds in her top seeming to become one with the cushions.

"I'm sorry if I was on edge earlier," she says. "It was quite a shock to have you in my house all of a sudden. And yet, I've been preparing for this for a long time. It was Alice I imagined sitting down with, truth be told, but sometimes these things skip a generation, I suppose."

Sadie gives Beth an encouraging glance, and she decides to be conciliatory. "Thanks for having us. And for being willing to talk."

"Is it okay if we leave any questions off until after dinner?" Julie asks. "For now, I suggest we relax. Get to know each other."

There is an awkward silence. Beth sips her wine, tasting the broad smack of it in the middle of her tongue. She has gained an appreciation for it, this last year. Sadie nuzzles the dog, who appears comatose.

"You're a dog person, clearly, Sadie," Julie ventures.

"Yeah. I'm mad about them."

"How about you, Beth?"

"I'm actually slightly allergic," says Beth. "But Princess is cute."

"Precious," Julie corrects her.

"The dog in *Silence of the Lambs* is called Precious," Sadie pipes up.

Julie nods. "Who do you think she's named after?"

They talk about their favorite films—a nice, neutral topic of conversation at which Sadie excels. Every so often Julie drifts back into the kitchen to check on something until she tells them it's time to eat. There is both roast chicken and roast beef; the chicken turns out to be for Precious.

"She won't eat dog food for me." Julie tears off a few chunks and tosses them on the floor; Precious tentatively licks them before swallowing them whole. "That'll do her a few days, now."

Sadie tries to help with the serving, but Julie insists that they both sit. She carves the beef and puts steaming dishes of dauphinoise potatoes and roasted vegetables on the table. They eat, and Beth grudgingly articulates at some point that it is delicious. Julie gives Sadie the run of the wine rack. They talk about easy things, like Dublin pubs and college and their ambitions for the future. Sadie's future, mainly; when Julie brings up swimming, Beth puts her fingers in her ears and starts to nonsense-sing loudly.

"It's a sore subject right now," Sadie explains.

"How do you even know about my swimming?"

Julie refills everyone's glass. "I follow your progress online. You hold a number of records, don't you?"

"I used to," Beth says, wary. "So you keep tabs on the whole family, do you?"

"Only the famous ones."

Beth allows herself to feel flattered for a moment. She glances across at Sadie, who is drunk and grinning; already thoroughly won over. *Don't lose focus.*

"You said no questions until after dinner," Beth begins. "I know it's late, so I'll just ask about one thing."

She can't shake the memory of Lydia just before she died, picking back over the day of Ben's death. *She got to play the widow.*

"Why did he drive all the way down here?" Beth asks.

Julie sighs heavily. "To protect Lydia, I dare say. To protect Alice. He didn't want them finding him."

"But he could have gone anywhere. Why here?"

"This place meant a lot to him."

"He didn't call to you first, or anything? He didn't leave any kind of message?"

"There was nothing, I'm afraid. No immediate warning signs. I hadn't spoken to Ben or Lydia for weeks—Lydia had withdrawn from me, and I supposed she'd brought Ben with her. Though I felt as if I was in constant dialogue with them, because I was transcribing the tapes I'd made that summer. Oh, and Jonathan and I were splitting up. So I had a lot going on."

"Do you wish, now, that you'd reached out to him?"

"Of course. But I was trying to get some perspective. I wondered, was this sort of arrangement sustainable? I hoped so but increasingly suspected not. And for me, that's what Roslyn was—that precise chemistry of time and place and opportunity, something that was not built to last. But, you know, on the day that Ben died I was happy, transcribing away. Ben was reflecting on poetry and what it meant to him. *You can't summarize a poem*, he was saying. *You can't adapt it into another form. It just is. It's a stubborn beauty.* And then he laughed. He must have been looking over at Lydia when he said that. I still have that on tape somewhere.

"Anyway, there was a knock on the door. I was so engrossed in the tape that I almost didn't answer. Peter, the local Garda, was on the doorstep. He would've given me lifts back from the village every now and then. Ben and Lydia too—he would have known them. And he said, 'I'm afraid I have bad news. There was a suicide earlier, a man jumped from the cliff. A witness is saying it was Ben Crowe.' I had to grab the door frame, to steady myself. *A poem is a moment snatched out of time*, Ben was saying on the tape. *Like letters; they're the only way of capturing how you felt at a particular point.*

"Peter drove me to the cliff in the driving rain. On the way we passed Ben and Lydia's car at the pier, and that was when I knew it was real. A rake of locals had gathered—rubbernecking, you know. The tide was in and you couldn't see a thing. They were trying to launch rescue boats but the sea was too rough. It was chaotic. I stayed out there while they searched. Have you contacted Lydia? I asked them. They had, she was on the way. There was a body down there all right, but the divers couldn't get to it. Eventually they told me to get in out of the rain, but I had to stay until she got there. I had to hold the fort. It was midnight by the time she arrived. No motorways in those days. And she had to borrow a car from someone."

"She said that even after she got here, people weren't sure which one of you was the widow."

"Did she say that? Oh, how ghastly." Julie tops up their wineglasses again. "I can assure you there was no confusion in *my* mind. I mainly remember the two of us huddled together on the cliff, in shock. They called off the search around two in the morning and I brought her back here. I hoped things would be as they had been in the summer—that we would sleep together, cry together. But she took the spare room. They recovered him in the morning, and I didn't see her again until the funeral. I thought I would suffocate in that little room with that closed coffin, that smiling framed photo of Ben propped up on the lid. There was Ben's father, with his creased, decent face. I'd never met him before but he was kind to me." She worries the stem of her glass with her long fingers. "I remember little Alice, too, in a new black dress with grazes on her knees. I ended up sitting with her for most of the wake. I wasn't able to handle much adult conversation."

"How was she?" Beth asks, leaning forward.

"She was a kid. Panicky and crying one minute, laughing and running around the next. She was confused. People kept being nice to her and giving her sweets and fizzy drinks, or else hugging her and crying and telling her that her daddy was gone to heaven. She told a few of them, sharply, that there was no such thing." Julie pauses. "Lydia tolerated Ben's religious belief, even admired its sincerity. But she was never going to let him raise their daughter a Catholic."

Julie's hand shakes slightly as she drinks.

"Alice has gone a bit religious now," Beth says. "She goes to Mass the odd time."

Julie smiles faintly. "That's interesting. Rebellion takes many forms."

"Was Ben's a church funeral?"

"Yes. Like a state occasion, almost. Lydia knew it's what Ben would have wanted, what his family would have wanted." She shudders. "Lydia nearly took the head off the priest when he said that Ben was at peace now. Like that was any consolation. Lydia wanted him with her—suffering, mad even. But with her, still."

*

Late in the night, Sadie asks about a local taxi service but Julie won't hear of it.

"You will take the converted barn," she says grandly. She is drunk; they all are.

They stumble outside on the crunchy gravel and bow their heads into the rain. A small outdoor light marks the door to the barn. It's as rugged inside as it is out. Thick stone walls, a fireplace, a lofted bed.

Julie looks at them fondly, framed by the blackness of the open doorway, and seems to be about to say something before leaving them. In the end, she just says, "Well, good night," and closes the heavy wooden door with a clatter.

Once under the covers, Beth begins to compose a long email to Justin, but falls asleep before she can press Send.

Chapter Eighteen

They're woken early by light pouring through a high east-facing window. Beth goes downstairs to retch in the bathroom. After that is done, the narrow steps back to the loft seem insurmountable. She calls Sadie down, asking her to please bring her shoes. As they cross the yard to the cottage, Beth realizes with alarm that there are holes in her memory of the previous night. The back door is unlocked. Beth can smell rashers crisping and the rich undertow of coffee. Julie is gliding about the galley kitchen, a talk show on the radio, humming to herself.

"Sleep well?" She doesn't wait for a response. "Sit yourselves down there."

They sit at the round table in the living room where they had dinner the night before. Beth moves her fingers reflexively to her temples. Her thoughts feel suspended in her head, like sediment trying to settle. Everything irritates, even Sadie grinding pepper onto her fried egg in three deliberate twists. Beth goes humbly to the kitchen for a large glass of water, and is relieved when nobody passes a remark.

When they've finished eating, Julie says, "I thought we'd start the day off with something a little less intense. Fun, even."

This turns out to be photographs: a thick leather-bound

photo album, sitting on the coffee table. Beth turns the pages with just the tips of her fingers, Sadie at her shoulder, fascinated. The photos are square and muted in color—the blues inky, the yellows mustard, the greens murky. They are summer scenes, mostly: ice-cream cones, sunglasses, figures crouching in the surf. The first figure she focuses on is Alice, a gap-toothed grin in every frame, though still with a foreshadowing of her adult self. There's Lydia, transformed by her eighties clothes and hair. Only Ben looks like he belongs in the photos, because he never made it out of the decade.

Beth stops on a page that contains photos of just Lydia and Julie. Lydia is beaming in every one of them and something crumples in Beth's chest. There they are posing for the camera outside a pub, unpacking a picnic, collecting shells on the beach.

Julie nods toward the photos. "We were beautiful once. Can you imagine that?"

Beth refuses to meet her gaze. "I always thought Lydia was beautiful."

Another page: just Ben this time. He's glowing in most of the pictures. Fine hair blowing in the breeze as he stands on the shore. Grinning in an apron with a set of barbecue tongs in his hand. Stretched out on an olive-green couch with a book, Lydia in an armchair next to him with a sheaf of paper and a pen. Both of them wearing small smiles. Though they aren't touching, they seem connected, as though they've just shared a private joke.

There's a photo of Julie with Ben, too. She seems to be

interviewing him, a Dictaphone on the table between them, but there's a sense that they've been asked to pose rather than been captured midconversation. There are no pictures of the three of them together. One of them was always behind the camera.

"He looks . . . happy." Beth is nonplussed.

"Everyone smiles in photos, dear. It's a Pavlovian response."

"It's not just the smile. He looks *good*. Tanned, healthy."

Sadie nods. "The story we've always heard is that he was half-demented when writing *Roslyn*."

Beth holds up the album, almost accusingly. "Six months later—five months, even?—he takes his own life. How can he be so happy?" Her words come out globular and wobbly. She feels Sadie's hand on her back and leans into it, grateful. "I know there's no good reason."

"It's not really about reason at all," Julie says. "I think it was pure animal instinct. Needing an escape."

"Escape from what?"

"His mind, dear, his own self. It wasn't the first thing he tried. He tried sleeping too much, drinking too much. Then drugs, legal or otherwise. Dying was always the last resort."

Beth looks back down at the photos. She's unknowingly been stroking Ben's head with her thumb.

"Does this make any sense?" Julie says, settling down on the other side of her. "Can you see how Ben might have been happy that summer? Because your friends can always make you happy, for a time anyway."

Beth pauses, trying for a different tack. "You wrote that he was bipolar. What made you think that was the case?"

"Well, his behavior was almost textbook. The manic episodes, the euphoria, the grandiosity, the bursts of inspiration. All of which, mind, made him an incredible companion. But then would come the depressive episodes, where he would lose his sense of pleasure in all things, lash out, be unable to work and hate himself for it."

Beth holds up her hands. "Look, I'm a first-year psychology student. I know how tempting it is to go around diagnosing people with various disorders. But it's dangerous, too."

"I see what you're saying. But you have to understand how people talked about Ben back then—they dismissed him as a madman, or a coward, or they spoke about him in hushed, reverent terms. Such a beautiful soul, he couldn't last long in this world, that sort of bullshit. I couldn't decide which reaction I hated more." Julie sighs. "Maybe it was presumptuous of me, but the manic depression was at least an explanation that made some sort of sense. He died of an illness. It happens. I even thought I was saving his reputation in some way. But Lydia didn't see it like that. She thought I was airing their dirty laundry. She'd made such a supreme effort, for so many years, to hide Ben's problematic behavior from the public. I wasn't always living in Ireland back then, and maybe I'd forgotten what attitudes to mental illness were like. You didn't talk about it. Ever."

"It's still not easy," Beth says. "Even now."

Sadie clears her throat, as if to remind them both that

she's still there. "Can I ask—what was your intention with the book? What were you hoping to achieve?"

It's a scholarly question, Beth thinks—the sort of thing that Justin might ask.

Julie thinks for a moment. "The critical studies I'd written before were about dead writers. Having a living, breathing subject who could answer my questions was quite novel. As was the fact that I was Ben's friend. I was concerned about that, at first—would I have the necessary authorial distance?"

"I was going to ask about that—the conflict of interest," Sadie says earnestly.

Julie pauses. "Quite. In the end, instead of fighting against my friendship with Ben, I decided to embrace it. I would get the interrogative part out of the way. I'd invite Ben, Lydia and Alice down to stay here, fire my questions at Ben, and then hole up on my own to sift through his answers and let the book unfold. Jonathan and I were slowly doing up the house. The barn was still a barn then, a ramshackle one, so Ben and Lydia slept upstairs and Alice took the box room. It was a great experiment, but somehow it worked beautifully. Everything seemed simple, like we could just all live here together indefinitely. The four of us here, like a family— and the odd cameo from my husband. He seemed like the visitor, not Ben and Lydia. I was happy. Your grandmother was happy, she told me so. Even little Alice was happy."

"Did she know what was going on?" Beth asks.

Julie shakes her head. "Of course we were discreet around her, and she was used to being dragged different places by her parents for work. Nothing seemed out of the ordinary for her. And Ben seemed to be thriving, especially as he approached the end of the draft of *Roslyn*. Everything seems so clear all of a sudden, he told me. Lines you would have agonized over, rewritten several times—you end up striking them out with joy in your heart. You see what the poem is meant to be, how it's been trying to reveal itself to you all along. He was so generous toward me as an interviewer. There was no question he wouldn't answer, no amount of time he wouldn't give to make sure I understood him correctly."

Julie looks down at the table a long time, begins to trace the grain with her finger. Beth is about to prompt her with another question when she speaks again.

"Everything changed when he died. I was grieving, I was drinking too much. I went from trying to deconstruct his work to trying to solve the riddle of his death. I ended up writing myself into the book. It felt like the only realistic thing to do." She looks Beth in the eye.

"Were you in touch with Lydia during the writing of it?"

Julie shakes her head. "I kept trying to reach out to fact-check things with her, but she wouldn't engage. And then, I've told you what happened when I sent her the manuscript." She pauses. "I did get through to her once, anyway. I rang her after midnight and caught her off guard. 'We killed him,' she said."

Sadie shivers.

"She thought Ben wouldn't have done it if it had meant abandoning her, leaving her on her own," Julie continues.

"But when she and I found happiness together, that gave him permission. *We* gave him permission."

In the afternoon, Julie drives to the nearest town to "pick up some bits for the dinner," leaving Beth and Sadie alone in the house. Beth lies down, gently shoving a grumbling Precious up to one end of the couch so that she can stretch out, while Sadie goes straight for the bookshelves.

". . . it all makes sense?" Sadie is saying. "The super-sexy bits of *Roslyn*, where he's describing women sexually but not in terms of *ownership* or domination, and how it's almost sapphic in its language . . . He was describing Lydia and Julie in *real time*, don't you see?"

"Can we not talk about them for a while?" Beth says weakly.

"Fine." Sadie deposits a pile of books on the coffee table with a bang and curls up in the armchair to read.

Beth dozes, or attempts to doze. She is brought back to the room by Precious licking her face experimentally. She sits up.

Sadie is looking at her, concerned. "You okay?"

"Yeah. Just . . . exhausted to be honest."

"Me too." Sadie yawns and stretches. "When this is all over, we'll head off to the sun somewhere. Jess and a few of the girls are thinking of heading to Barcelona in August. Will you come? We can recover from all of this, okay? Just chill."

The prospect of going on a girly sun holiday with Sadie's friends does not sound relaxing to Beth. It would consist of nothing but sunbathing on crowded beaches and drinking and going out dancing. Karaoke was likely.

"Thanks, Sades. I'd only ruin your fun, though." *Failed Olympians are bad at holidays,* she wants to say. *We're no good at dancing. We can't do fancy things to our hair, only push it under our skullcaps, or leave it down until it drip-dries.*

"Don't be ridiculous."

"I'll just make everyone nervous." She imagines herself doing laps in the pool while everyone else suns themselves on the deck. "Besides, they're your friends, not mine."

"Jess is your friend. *I'm* your friend. Even when you do your annoying tough loner act and try to alienate me."

"Okay, noted. Thanks, Sadie." She gets up, walks over to the bookshelves. "Anything interesting here?"

"Loads of awesome American editions."

All of Julie's own scholarly works are on a shelf to themselves, near the door; Beth goes over for a closer look. She runs her finger along the shelf, across *Comely Maidens,* across books about John Berryman, Willa Cather, Dorothy Parker, across the spines of thick anthologies and academic journals.

"Take whatever you like."

Beth jumps, almost guiltily. Julie is standing in the doorway, several strained-looking shopping bags dangling from each hand. Sadie jumps up to help her.

"To keep, I mean," Julie adds. "Doesn't have to be one of mine, either. You too, Sadie."

"Really? Class." Sadie carries the groceries through to the galley kitchen.

Julie looks as if she might follow, then hesitates. She locks eyes with Beth. "There's something else I've been meaning to show you."

She settles the one remaining bag in her hand on the ground; there is a distinct *clink*. She walks over to the mid-century writing desk tucked neatly against the wall, and takes something from the drawer. She crosses the room to Beth, holding it out.

It's an eighty-page lined copybook with a picture of a round tower on the cover.

Beth opens it, and she understands nothing. Ben's writing is tiny, cramped, crabbed. It goes in all directions. On the lines, but also in the margins, upside down, up the sides. Stuff angrily crossed out. Groups of numbers circled. She leafs through the pages, looking for some kind of sense, but nothing comes.

"You might want some privacy for this," Julie says.

Beth takes the copybook up into the eaves of the barn, and begins to read. It seems crucial not to cry, and she focuses on this task, looking at the pages until her vision becomes blurry. The syntax initially makes no sense. It takes her a while to realize that he skipped lines, and then, when he ran out of space, went back to the start and wrote in the lines he'd skipped. An unintentional code. She wonders why he didn't simply start a new copybook. Did the local shop not have the type he wanted? Or did he know, on some level, that this was his last record?

She stares at the cramped pages, willing sense into them. The word "Roslyn" appears many times, in hard, scribbly capitals. Occasionally there is an initial—L for Lydia, or A for Alice. Beth breathes deeply until she's calm. Goes back to the start of the journal and tries again.

She spends about an hour with it, copying down a few phrases into the back of her own notebook:

It's simply the other side. Stepping over a door saddle. The thinnest of membranes.

I worry about the botched communication of it. The intended message is rarely the one received.

"Leavetaking"—too grandiose? Too maudlin?

Is it one's right to simply take oneself away? I do not mean to suggest it's like leaving a dreary party or storming out of an argument, BUT.

My poet self is not my best self. But there's no getting away from him.

Tired, tired, so fucking tired.

Julie is chopping vegetables when Beth enters the kitchen. She had hoped to throw down the gauntlet somehow, but all she can do is hold up the copybook helplessly.

"Why do you have this?" Beth's voice is quiet. "Someone told me that Lydia destroyed the diaries."

Julie puts down the knife, meets her gaze. "She did, to the best of my knowledge. The ones that were in your house at least. He left this one behind, that summer." She takes a step closer.

Beth hugs the journal to her chest. "I'm keeping this."

Julie looks stricken, but nods. "You should have it. It's Ben's, after all."

She looks down at it. "This is as close as he came, isn't it. To an explanation."

"I think so."

She meets Julie's eye. "You should have given it to Lydia. She deserved to see this."

"I know. But I was afraid. She'd already told me she was going to burn the others . . . and I didn't think she'd want to read those words."

"You made the decision for her."

"Yes, I suppose I did."

On the third day, Julie suggests a walk. Beth, suffering from a cumulative hangover, welcomes the blast of sea air. They trudge along on the wet, packed sand, with the occasional shell or crab carcass crunching underfoot.

"So, who had the power in the relationship?"

"It felt equal."

"Come on. No relationship is, even when there's only two people involved."

"All right then. Your grandmother, I suppose. She was married to Ben, and she and I . . . well, I was closer to her than I was to him."

"Did you love Ben?"

"Yes. But toward the end, it was rarely just the two of us."

"What about you and Lydia?"

"We were alone together a lot," she says, simply. "Ben drew me in. But it was for Lydia I stayed."

The ocean washes closer, whispery, as if to shush them. Huge gulls circle over their heads.

"Was Lydia gay, then?" Beth says slowly, trying to keep her voice steady. "Is that why she never remarried? Was she closeted?" The Lydia in her mind is going from fierce and independent to fearful and repressed, and she hates it.

"I'd been with women before. She hadn't. Stop me if this gets strange for you." Julie puts her hands in the pockets of her coat, a heavy wool thing, unseasonable for this time of year. "I admired her, but not in that way, at first. I thought she was poised, clever, gracious. And I was intrigued by the way she handled Ben. She loved him, and was so proud of him, but if he started to get boorish or rowdy, she would step in and manage the situation. Soothe frayed tempers. Turn what he'd said into a joke."

"Sounds exhausting."

"It was. But she made it look easy. I was in awe of her. I was surprised she wanted to be my friend."

"Because Ben wanted you."

Julie nods. "Anyone else would have shunned me or belittled me. Anyone else would have been *threatened*. Not Lydia. Maybe it was a case of keeping your enemies closer, but . . ."

She is looking out to sea, speaking to the waves.

"I know I said it was an idyllic summer, but it didn't start out like that. When they arrived, Ben was in a bad way. He was drinking pretty heavily, blacking out on occasion. He was never physically violent, but he was unpredictable. Lydia was just glad to have another person around to help. The first night, he got so drunk he went out onto the porch and started smashing the empties. We were both too scared to go out and stop him. I showed

Lydia their room upstairs and all we could hear was the tinkle of glass, Ben roaring into the night. We both started laughing and wound up crying, holding each other on the bed. Some nights he'd disappear and we'd know he was on a bender somewhere in the village, and when he'd roll in drunk Lydia would crawl into my bed, like a scared child."

"Is that how it started?"

"Yes. Comfort. It was only on the nights when Ben was messy. And in the mornings he'd be apologetic, like a sweet old bear with a sore head. We felt terrible. When he found out—well, you don't need to know the details. He walked in on us. And I remember this jolt of sheer terror, just here." She indicates her throat. "But he was fine. Surprised, a bit tense, but not angry. He joined us sometimes but he seemed to sense that Lydia and I needed time alone, too. After a while he was teasing us, even writing about us. 'Feast of the Assumption' is about us."

"He was never jealous?"

"He was a big-hearted, open-minded man, your grand-father. And God knows, Lydia tolerated *his* affairs. He told us we didn't have to hide our feelings anymore. But we did, for some reason. I suppose because Jonathan visited occa-sionally. We didn't want him suspecting anything, though he did find out eventually."

Beth thinks of the passage in the book where Lydia and Jonathan disappeared together one night, Julie describing her jealousy. Beth had assumed that it was Jonathan who Julie was scared of losing.

"But you know what? Ben stopped drinking, the very

weekend he found out about Lydia and me. And for the rest of the summer, everything was harmonious. In the morning, we worked—Lydia on *Red Gate Review*, me on the book, Ben on *Roslyn*. He broke through whatever rut he was in. In the evening we'd have dinner and I'd ask them all sorts of questions with the Dictaphone running. And later Lydia would climb the stairs and either go to Ben's room or to mine. And everything was right in the world." She pauses. "That sort of precarious happiness, it's not built to last. Even with the best will in the world."

They come to a sandy bluff with gentle slopes. Julie begins to climb up a well-worn path, and Beth follows her. When they crest the headland, they come to a wooden bench looking out to sea. Julie sits, and gestures to Beth to join her. The wooden slats burn the bare undersides of Beth's thighs, reminding her of the sauna. Between them on the bench is a brass plaque.

" 'In memory of Benjamin Crowe,' " Beth reads. "There's one of these near home, too."

"I had them erected about twenty years ago. A gesture of guilt, I suppose." Julie keeps facing the sea, watching the waves swell and crash. "You know, you remind me of her. I see her stubbornness in you. A certain . . . forgive me, intractability."

Beth smiles a little. "I wonder what I've inherited from Ben. I keep asking myself if there's something self-destructive about me, too. And then I think about 'Dark Vein,' you know. 'From my mother's mother's mother.' "

"Or in your case, I suppose, your mother's father's mother."

She nods. "Maybe there's no escaping it. The self-destructive streak."

"Or maybe, because you understand your history, you're better equipped to find your way forward." She smiles sideways at Beth. "I'm glad you read the biography. It's quite possibly the only copy, outside of my home. What do you plan to do with it?"

"I haven't thought that far ahead yet." But she already knows she will give it to Sadie.

She answers the phone to her mother. It's a video call, unusual for Alice.

"I thought it'd be nice to have a look at you," she says.

They exchange how-are-yous, which Beth sustains only briefly before coming clean. "I'm not in Laois."

Alice's smile slips. The worry is always there, Beth realizes, just beneath the surface. "Where are you?"

"We went on a road trip," Beth says in a rush. "We're in West Cork."

"I see." Her eyes flit, taking in the whole screen, as though she could divine the truth of Beth's statement from the wall behind her head.

Beth swallows. This is what she hates about video calls—her emotions are visible. "I came to visit Julie."

Alice's face twitches. Beth knows her well enough to understand that this is hurt, not anger. "Why?" she asks quietly.

"I had to, Mum. I needed to know more."

"When are you planning on coming back? Gran's birthday is the day after tomorrow, remember?"

Beth says nothing. She'd forgotten about the birthday, about their plans, about everything.

"Well—look. We won't scatter her without you," Alice says. "But I'm not comfortable with you being out there. It's an isolated place and I've not even met the woman—"

"You spent a summer with her!"

"I was a child."

They are silent for a moment. Beth catches sight of her furrowed face in the bottom corner of the screen. She is reminded of how sometimes, in the mirrored wall of a changing room, she doesn't recognize her own reflection.

"She's not what you think," Beth says finally.

"She's manipulative, Beth. You wouldn't know what she'd be saying to you."

Beth can see the pain in her mother's face, the discomfort, but the one thing she doesn't see is surprise. "She's not lying to me, Mum. She and Lydia—they loved each other."

"Until they didn't," Alice says flatly.

Beth stares at the small screen, gets a sudden urge to touch it, as if she could really reach out. "You knew."

Her mother sighs. "There wasn't much your gran kept from me."

"Why didn't you *tell* me?"

Alice's face on the small screen looks genuinely mystified. "What business was it of yours?"

In the morning, she knows that she has to go home. When she tells Sadie and Julie about the scattering of Lydia's ashes, Julie looks at her with unguarded hope.

"I don't suppose . . . Could I come with you? It would mean so much."

It doesn't seem possible to refuse.

Beth goes for a long walk by herself while Julie and Sadie prepare their last dinner in the cottage. She wants to get a feel for the magic of the place, for the transcendent feeling her grandfather found here. It eludes her, even though she loves the small black faces of the sheep in the fields, the tangy taste of the sea, the basking sharks in the distance.

She is on the front porch, her face upturned to the breeze off the ocean, when she feels an embrace from behind. She relaxes, thinking first of Justin, then of Ben. When she looks down, it's Julie's large lined hands holding her. Beth remains perfectly still in the charge of the moment. It's as if Julie is trying to impress something on her, something that can't be communicated with words or even eye contact. It is probably only seconds but feels longer. Julie goes back inside without saying a word.

From the passenger seat, Beth catches Julie's eye in the rearview mirror and looks away, suddenly self-conscious. But Sadie has no sooner pulled out onto the road than Julie wraps her coat around herself and slumps down in her seat, unknowable under a black eye mask. There is something ominous about this, and Beth is half-afraid that she will not be able to wake Julie up. As soon as they hit the M50, however, Julie is sitting up again and perfectly alert.

Her mother comes out to the driveway to greet them.

Beth texted to forewarn her that Julie was coming, and Alice looks uncharacteristically flustered. She hugs Beth fiercely, then Sadie too, thanking her for driving them home safely. After a moment's hesitation, she shakes Julie's hand, which transitions into an awkward arm-pat when Julie tears up. Beth stands between them, watchful. Julie keeps thanking her and apologizing and Alice keeps replying *No worries* with grim determination.

When they sit down for coffee, Sadie drives the conversation, telling Alice all about herself. Beth looks at her with gratitude. *Will you stay over?* she mouths, and Sadie beams in response. As Beth and Alice make small talk, warming up to one another again, Julie wanders the house like a ghost. "It hasn't changed a bit," she says every so often. Alice allows her to drift through the rooms; they sit at the table with their mugs and wait for her to circle back to them.

After finishing her coffee Julie asks, "Have you nothing stronger?"

Beth opens a bottle of wine and leaves it on the table, where Alice and Julie are already examining the photo album. She and Sadie slip out and leave them to it.

Later that evening, Alice brings Beth into the study. While she was away, Alice had brought a librarian from the National Library into the house to make an assessment of Ben's archive.

A number of objects are spread out on the study table, like museum pieces. Treasures that Beth had overlooked in her hurried search of the boxes. An old-fashioned pair of glasses. A fat, expensive-looking pen. A lighter. A silk handkerchief with B.C. stitched into the corner. Beth is almost afraid to touch them, but her mother fingers each one lovingly.

"These bring me back," she says. "I can *see* him with these things. He was a big ball of energy, my dad."

They stop for a moment, looking at the small spread of objects, the remnants of Ben's life. Beth picks up a set of rosary beads. "Were these his?"

Alice nods. "They were in his pocket when he was found."

Beth fingers the beads carefully. They're pewter, beautiful in their plainness.

"Keep them," says Alice.

Beth is balling the beads in her fist, letting them slip from one hand to the other. "Oh, no. You should have them."

Alice shakes her head when Beth tries to give them back. "Hang on to them. If you'd like, that is."

Beth takes them. She owns nothing of Ben's. Maybe it's morbid, but she wants them. She wants them snug in her own pocket.

What would have been Lydia's eightieth birthday dawns cloudless. Beth wakes early, the way she used to at the height of her training, and goes downstairs to make a fry-up for four.

At nine o'clock, Beth, Sadie, Alice and Julie get in the car and drive to the pier. Beth sits in the passenger seat with the sturdy oak box in her hands. They pull up in the car park and for a moment, the whole thing feels rushed; Beth frets that she should have texted Pearse, should have invited more people, should have made more of a ceremony out of it. But listening to her mother and Julie talking quietly about the morning, about the streak of good weather, she knows how rare this is.

They walk to the end of the pier as three generations, three overlapping timelines. Beth thinks of what she might say if she met herself, a year younger, walking the promenade. You will be humbled, she would say. You will suffer. You'll lose Lydia. You will fall in love and you'll walk away. You will reckon with your failure and learn to love the water again. You will read poetry. You will go on the trail of a suicide and find a love story instead.

For such a bright, clear morning, there isn't a single jogger on the pier. They are alone, the four of them, where Lydia stood decades before to scatter Ben's ashes. Alice slides open the box and lets the wind take Lydia, the ashes winding in an arc out to sea. *A comet appeared.* What is a comet but ice and ash and dust?

Beth doesn't want the ritual to be over just yet. Seized by an old impulse, she pulls at the collar of her summer dress, yanking it over her head; she toes away her flats. Julie looks at her, alarmed; Sadie starts laughing; Alice hisses the words *Beth, what are you doing?* But her bare feet are sure on the warm concrete and she's moving forward, launching herself over the edge of the pier, her legs pedaling the air. She hits the water, plummeting into those dark blue folds that always looked to her like another country, impossible to come back from. As soon as she tastes salt, her body responds and she shoots to the surface, breaking into daylight. Sadie is still laughing and her mother is waving and Beth is breathing, kicking, plunging under again.

Acknowledgments

The Silent Woman by Janet Malcolm and *Swimming Studies* by Leanne Shapton were both instrumental in the early development of this novel. *The Silent Woman* made me want to write about biography, archives and legacy, and *Swimming Studies* brilliantly portrays the tension between competitive and recreational sport. The scene where Marina practices her race on the hotel bed was inspired by *Swimming Studies*. The Benjamin Crowe poem described in chapters 7–8 owes a debt to the unforgettable Don Paterson poem "The Lie," from his collection *Rain*.

My heartfelt thanks to the following:

Everyone at Sandycove, especially Brendan Barrington for his investment and belief, and for elevating the story to another level. Holly Ovenden for the wonderful jacket, and Mary Chamberlain for her care with the manuscript.

Lucy Luck, for her brilliant suggestions on the initial draft, and for advocating for this book from the beginning.

The Arts Council, for providing vital support at various stages of my career. Cill Rialaig and the Tyrone Guthrie Centre, Annaghmakerrig, where early portions of this book were written. The Ó Bhéal Winter Warmer Festival, where I first read from this novel as a work-in-progress. To the editors who published stories and essays of mine while I was working on this book—thank you.

To every friend who offered feedback and encouragement along the way, in particular Laura Cassidy, Olive Coffey, Danny Denton, Claire Hennessy, Ailbhe Ní Ghearbhuigh and Billy Ramsell.

The Ryan family—Séamus, Ber, Conor and Eileen—for their unwavering love and support.

Finally, to Cal Doyle, who makes everything feel possible.